NEW WOMEN'S FICTION

NEW WOMEN'S FICTION

Edited by Aorewa McLeod

New Women's Press
Auckland

Published by New Women's Press Ltd,
P.O. Box 47-339, Auckland, New Zealand

ISBN 0 908652 30 5

Cover illustration by Kathryn Madill
Cover type by Neysa Moss
Typeset by Glenfield Graphics Ltd, Auckland

Printed through All Round Book Productions

Contents

Introduction

I've always thought that anthologies of stories told me more about the editor's concept of fiction than they did about the representative quality of the stories chosen. However, I read over 250 stories submitted for the collection (they had to be previously unpublished) and I tried to choose stories that, for me, suggested the range of possibilities for women's writing. These are not the best stories according to a particular concept of good stories. They're a mixture of the stories that affected me most, that suggested there are many different ways of expressing ourselves as women, and that demonstrated the many and various voices women can use. Reading Ngahuia Te Awekotuku, Sylvia Mary Bowen, Wendy Pond, Rawinia White, Fran Marno, Carin Svensson I hear different and clearly defined voices speaking.

Speaking. I've taught a course on Women Writers for eight years. Every year we talk about whether there is such a thing as a woman's style, a woman's way of writing, separate from subject matter. Usually we end up saying, – well – that women write within the dominant patriarchal cultural mode. But I argue that one way women contradict the hegemonic cultural models is in their use of orality. Women gossip, women tell the stories to their children. Women writers seem to be closer to oral tradition and its possibilities, in opposition to the formal high culture of their society.

Many of these fictions are short. But many of these writers are beginning writers. For many it's the first piece they've had published, for a few it's the first finished piece they've written. I see this collection as a book of beginnings, a collection of short fictions whose variety might suggest that there's no correct format for a story. What excited me most about editing this collection was putting the stories together at the end – the contrasts and juxtapositions of voices and modes. For me, the final effect is different from the individual merits of any one story. I'd like this collection to say to women writers in Aotearoa – 'You're in a very exciting position – don't write stories like everyone else – don't give a damn about whether *The Listener* or *Metro* or *Islands* will publish it now or what sort of topic will win the American Express

Short Story Award.' Hulme and Grace have shown us that we, as women in a post-colonial culture, can have a distinctive and unique voice and point of view, and we'll get there.

I could wish there were more stories by Maori women and from Pacific Island women. But almost all the stories submitted were by Pakeha women, reflecting the fact that we are not an integrated bi-cultural or multi-cultural society. Kiri Potaka-Dewes said, about the lack of Maori participation in the Women's Studies Association publications, 'Maori women were not likely to be happy about its appearance in a Pakeha publication. They believe that their information and knowledge is Maori and should remain totally under their control.' I thank Arapera Hineira, Ngahuia Te Awekotuku and Rawinia White who have allowed me to include their stories.

Virginia Woolf in her classic *A Room of One's Own* wrote of the position of a middle-class white woman in a patriarchal culture: 'If one is a woman one is often surprised by a sudden splitting off of consciousness . . . when from being the natural inheritor of that civilization, she becomes on the outside of it, alien and critical.' She suggests woman has a double vision – she both belongs to the culture, and is an outsider. I begin this collection with Barbara Rea's 'Story' because it seems to me to express that condition so acutely, and in an area – the medical profession's control of women's bodies – that we have become so aware of since Coney and Bunkle. And Marvynne Sotheran's 'A Body like That' exemplifies the dilemma of how a woman can find herself other than as the object, the desired or abused focus of the gaze of the male. How does a woman find herself as subject? A speaking subject? This, for me, is what these stories are about – what it is like being a woman, and how can I find a voice and format to express it? Heather McPherson looks back to Gertrude Stein who did find a voice and a format. The protagonist of Fran Marno's 'Blood' wonders how she can write a story which expresses her physicality as a woman in a mode appropriate to the late eighties amongst the multiplicity of feminist discourses. She sees post-modernism, post-feminism as being capitulations to the dominant male discourse. But how can she avoid being read as a naive seventies feminist?

There are what might at first seem to be a disproportionate number of stories about lesbians, or by lesbians. But, possibly because of their position as outsider in a comparatively heterogeneous heterosexual society, New Zealand lesbians have been able to find a voice for woman as speaking subject, not as viewed object. Like Woolf's outsider woman, the lesbian here has no culture of her own and must find her own position and voice.

Anne Kennedy, in a review of the first *New Women's Fiction* in *The Listener* wrote: 'as current fiction there is a lack of freshness about it . . . a not very remarkable collection . . . There are no post-modern Milly's here . . . Documentary style is a thread running through *New Women's Fiction*.' Although Kennedy's review says no more than has often been said in academic critical debate about fiction ever since the death of the novel was announced back in the fifties, the immediate and personally outraged response to it by women writers and readers suggests that realism versus post-modernism is still a very alive issue in New Zealand today. While the humanist-realist Sargeson tradition certainly has been, and still is prevalent in short story writing, I agree with Kennedy that we can be trapped and limited by the realist mode, that we need to feel free to write in other ways. So, for this collection, I deliberately chose a wide range of styles and approaches, including a story by Kennedy.

I recognize that realism is in itself a literary convention, that the concept of fiction that we have is a product of an Anglo-Saxon bourgeois culture. But most of us, as readers, want and need the realistic mode. We've grown up with realism, we think it, we want it in our fictions, and what excites me is what our writers do with it to startle and provoke our readers. The formalist surrealism of South American writers, the post-modernism of French novelists is alien to most of us as readers. A friend, Jill, reading a recent avant-garde Australian collection of women's stories said to me: 'I can't stand these stories – they don't end. They have no endings.'

'Perhaps that's what life is like,' I said.

'Sure, but that's not what I want in a story. Stories leave you feeling satisfied at the end. They have beginnings, middles and ends.'

I recognize this yearning. I teach nineteenth-century fiction because I know and share that need for the story. But I also know that many of these stories I've chosen have no ending, no story. They're not satisfying. They're upsetting or they're confusing, or they leave you up in the air. If they work it's because they disturb. They won't give Jill what she wants but they might give us a sense of excitement, of possibilities.

Kennedy wrote of the two stories in the first collection that she liked: 'They are the only true feminist stories in that they are of the self as subject.' In the others the author stands back and watches herself –

as she has been taught to do.' And she added of the biographies at the end of the first collection: 'Even in "Autobiography" women do not see themselves as subject.' For me the post-modernist versus realist argument is most clearly spelt out in the response in New Zealand to the works of Janet Frame. A recent thesis by Brigid Carroll discusses the fact that Frame in her autobiographies presents 'the one character in all her writing (herself) who manages to develop innovations in language, and feelings about herself in society to an extent where she finds her freedom.' Carroll suggests that the popularity of the auto-biographies and the public recognition that Frame has achieved since their publication is related to the fact that they record the journey of a central persona, who creates a self as subject, and they reject the symbolic formalism of the novels for the metonymic mode of a seemingly realistic account of the interaction of self and the historical/social context.

Many New Zealanders who have read the autobiographies with pleasure have not, and never will, enjoy Frame's later novels. So while in my head I agree with the concept of a fiction that is self-reflective and aware of its own fictionality, in my gut I read for those stories that give me the impression 'Yes – that's what it must have been like!' – stories that move me or upset me. Back in 1970, when I was interviewed for the job I now hold in the Auckland University English Department, they asked me why I thought teaching English literature was worthwhile. I think I said something like 'It's vicarious experience – it's learning and understanding how others live and feel.' If I said that now they wouldn't give me the job. But I still believe this is why most of us read stories. I'd now add that we can also learn from reading how to write. I'd like to feel that this collection shows women that there's no right way to write, that no one writes like you, and that the way you write is fine if it talks to someone else. For me, the value of a collection like this is that it allows women to try it out, and allows other women to see what is possible.

Thanks to Mary Paul and Pat Rosier for reading some of the stories and giving me their opinions. Particular thanks to Wendy Harrex of New Women's Press for guiding me with unfailing good humour through the intricacies of editing.

AOREWA McLEOD

BARBARA REA

Story

> *'Lizzie Borden with an axe*
> *gave her father forty whacks'*

That may seem a funny way to start a communication such as this, but I've just this minute finished a book, by Angela Carter, it's short stories and the last one is called *The Fall River Axe Murders,* it's about a girl, well a woman really, who did something beyond understanding, just as you may think I have but anyway she hacked her old man to pieces with an axe, horrific you may say but if you read right through to the end of the story you can see just why she did it. It's a story about a woman with no way out. She writes so well, Angela Carter, she describes the Borden home so you could believe you were actually living in it yourself:

> *'One peculiarity of this house is the number of doors the rooms contain and, a further peculiarity, how all these doors are always locked. A house full of locked doors that open only into other rooms with other locked doors, for, upstairs and downstairs, all the rooms lead in and out of one another like a maze in a bad dream.'*

Like I say, I've just finished reading it, I came home today determined to get things under control, everything seems to be slipping lately, crashing round my head, breaking into fragments, or at least to sort out the house, really everything is a mess, I'm hopeless, the unwashed clothes flow out of the laundry like lava and as you came in you may have glanced through the kitchen door and noticed the roasting pan with the chicken grease floating on top? So, as I turned the key in the lock I said to myself, now, you have to do something about all this, you've come to the end of the road, you know what you must do, but I procrastinated, tried to give myself the slip, to delay the inevitable, and I sloped into the spare bedroom, it gets the afternoon sun, the sun was thick, oppressive in the room, I unlocked the french doors and stepped on to the verandah. The cat, our fat cat, was curled up, blissful,

among the dead oak leaves. When I say our cat I mean my cat, Don
doesn't like cats. Then I came in and lay down on the bed,

> *'now I lay me down to sleep*
> *I pray the Lord my soul to keep*
> *if I should die before I wake'*

the new curtains in this room look lovely, don't you think? Chintz,
a nice candy-stripe, a friend made them for me but, stupid of me, I
got far too much material, she made these cushions from the leftovers
but still there is this long strip of fabric, wasted, no use to anyone but
anyway I came home this afternoon and plumped up the new cushions
and settled down for a read. *Black Venus,* cover to cover. I picked
the book up at random out of the library. I do that sometimes when
I'm really desperate, maybe desperate is too strong a word? It's just
that in my bad days it seems that books are the only hope, no, that's
far too dramatic; Don says I am getting better he says he can perceive
each depressive episode is less incapacitating than the one before and
of course the pills he prescribes help, I know they do, it's just that they
kind of smudge everything up, I seem to be looking at my life through
grey cotton wool. 'Episode', that's the word he uses for the days when
the big black sack slides down over my face and I lie in bed feeling
like I'm hanging by my bleeding fingernails over the edge of the cliff,
there are people up there, at the top, sitting in the sunshine, laughing
together but they can't see me and it's too late because I'm falling, there
are cruel rocks down there, black and I'm down and down and but
what I meant to say is when I'm like that I just go into the library and
pick a name at random from the index, it's ridiculous I know but there's
a chance that someday I might find the right book, the one with the
answer, like someday my prince will come, just fairy stories, like the
stories by Angela Carter, she gives Bluebeard a mention more than once.
My favourite fairy story is about Portia, at least I know it's not strictly
a fairy story but her turning into a lawyer is so much more practical
somehow than into a princess or something. Even if she has to turn
back into a pumpkin in the end, like all the other stories, it's just what
she gets to say, you know about the quality of mercy et cetera.

I should mention the dream at this point. We had a late night last
night, Don took out this visiting overseas doctor, and his wife, he's
an expert in his field, Don says, so when I woke in an anxious twist,
early, early this morning in the dark, I lay there not moving for ages,
not wanting to disturb Don, he works such long hours at the hospital,

he needs all the sleep he can get but I must have dozed off eventually,
I dreamed . . .

*I'm taking a little dog for a walk or maybe it's a cat, it's small and
furry and cuddly and keeps jumping up wanting to be carried, like
a baby, but it slips out of its noose, I mean its collar, running on
to the road, oh no, I must save her, I go into the pet shop where
all these leads and collars are lined up on the counter but they look
so hard and cruel with metal studs and nails and tight unforgiving
leather but then I see one oh yes that's for me, soft, such nice colours,
stripes and this will do but then all hope is gone, I see her, they've
got her stretched out, on a rack, her paws tied up in hooks, this isn't
a pet shop it's a torture chamber, she's in agony, not dead yet just
looking at me mute I can't bear it but it's too late because something's
being pulled down over my head, I realize that after all the collar
is for me, I can feel it tighten round my throat . . .*

Dreams are overrated. That was last night, after our evening out.
I had hurried home from my university class, well, that sounds more
high-powered than it really is, it's not *real* university, just the Continuing
Education Department, twice a week, in the afternoon, it's mainly
housewives in the class, Don thought it would be a good idea, you may
as well fill your hours productively, Don said, I know I'm lucky, it's
a privilege, really, I don't know how I'd manage without him. The
course is called 'North American Women Writers of the Twentieth
Century', quite a mouthful, and yesterday we were doing Margaret
Atwood, I hadn't read anything of hers before, one of the handouts
was a short piece called 'Liking Men', I didn't really understand, it was
about how the writer, Margaret Atwood, thinks she knows a man and
then something happens, she looks at him again and suddenly he's
turned into a monster, like she says:

*'How can you like men? Still you continue to believe it can be done.
If not all men, at least some, at least two, at least one.'*

Anyway, as I was saying, I seem to be having some trouble reaching
the point with this, last night I dashed home from the class and found
Don ready to leave and I quickly got changed as he went as usual
through the house, along the hall, into all the rooms, locking all the
doors, snapping the bolts shut in all the windows and doors . . .

'a house full of locked doors

*the doors are always locked
like a maze in a bad dream'*

and then we went to pick up the visiting overseas expert and his wife,
and his wife, and his . . .

Dr Fraser and his wife collected Dr Crawford and his wife at their hotel
and drove through the pelting rain across the harbour bridge to the
restaurant. It was getting dark, Mary was thinking that, through the
water streaming down the windscreen, the glitter of the oncoming
headlights would soon be all that she could see. Most of Dr Fraser's
departmental colleagues were there already, in the snug room that had
been set aside for them. All the introductions going on, Mary trying
desperately to remember everybody's name, she knows she's met them
all at some hospital do or other, and this is Lucy Crawford from
Winnipeg, do you know –? Gulping gratefully at her first gin, and her
second, obviously the restaurant was making sure it milked the
maximum bar profits out of them before they would be allowed to eat.
But when they were all finally seated Mary was glad to find herself
placed beside Gary, nice Gary, on her left and Michael, whom she
doesn't know very well, he's been in Don's department only a few
months since returning from doing research in the States and Michael
on her right is saying how he's horrified by the light sentences given
to these people, what about that piece of scum convicted lately of
murdering that little girl, he'd been in prison but they released him,
let him back into the community to abuse more little girls until of course
at last he'd murdered one of them and he should be hanged, don't you
agree Mary? Mary drains her glass, it seems everyone is waiting for
her to say something and she starts to talk, she says that what's struck
her about this whole outcry is how the publicity about the abuses of
all these little girls has seemed to be cathartic to so many New Zealand
women and it's as if every woman who was interfered with when she
was a child is now standing up and saying and asking, revenge, it's all
come back to them, as if they realize at last they're allowed to be angry?
Down the table, Mary can see her husband Don looking uneasy, worried
that she might say too much, that she might start to tell a story about
an occasion long ago and far away when she met a man in a dark alley
but of course she's not going to blab all that out now what does he
take her for and she hears her voice say as she raises her newly-filled
wine glass, but, as a committed liberal, I have to say that hanging's

not the answer. I'd castrate the bastards first. Everyone laughs. They think she's joking.

> '*Lizzie Borden with an axe*
> *gave her father . . .*'

Now someone is talking about how he does some part-time counselling and how he can tell a woman who has been abused in the past the minute she walks in the door, and there are so many of them, a huge number, they are everywhere. Mary asks him, she can't remember his name, what is it, her husband has told her – Kendrick? Michael? no, that's Michael on her right but what counselling is this, she asks him, is it at the hospital and he replies no, he's a member of a church, it's work he does for the love of the Lord Jesus Christ and she remembers now, she had been told that there was a jesus freak in the department, as he says it's not possible to point at the men who do these things and say they are evil because every man has the same capacity, the same capacity to do evil. Mary asks, so you don't think it's a question of sexual politics, then, it's simply a matter of good and evil and someone's voice, the table has gone quiet, they're all listening, says, 'Watch out, Jonathan (that's his name, Jonathan) Mary's a bit of a feminist' and she can see from his face that the word feminist has the same effect on him as the words jesus freak have on her, he's defensive, but she needs to know the answer to her question, good and evil are suddenly important to her. 'Do you believe in redemption, then, Jonathan? Do you believe that men who do these things can be redeemed?' but she sees he thinks she's laughing at him and so do the others but she's not, she really needs to know, as if it were a matter of her own personal survival. He starts up again about the love of the Lord Jesus et cetera and there's no point, she turns to her right, to Michael, separate little conversations are breaking out again all over the table, she asks Michael if when he was in the States he'd ever come across any North American Women Writers, maybe –. No, says Michael, he never gets time to read books, after working all day at the hospital all the reading he does is to try to keep up with the medical literature and Mary replies that her husband is just the same, if she's lucky she can get him to read one novel a year. How many do you read, then, he asks. Well, she has to read two at least every week for this course she's doing at the university, not a proper university course, at least not for a degree or anything, it's a Continuing Education thing, and it all adds up, she feels she should apologize for this self-indulgence, he looks as though she's boring him rigid, she says of course she doesn't remember the half of them, she probably doesn't absorb or understand very much of the books she reads and what was the research he was doing in Boston exactly? 'Cats,' he replies. He can't have heard her. She repeats herself. He gives the same response, adding 'and dogs sometimes too'. What does he mean, but he's telling her now, he was conducting certain tests on them, experiments, they had to be fully aware throughout the procedure, so he could only give them local anaesthetic and then he'd introduce various substances into their, to see if, then he'd take his measurements on his machines, he's got nine publications out of it, not bad for a one-year fellowship. Mary nods and asks what happened to them, to the cats and dogs, after. He says he'd had to give up with the dogs in the end, they were so drippy, they'd get to recognize and trust the lab staff and they'd lie there, on their backs, still conscious and they'd start to wag their tails at the lab staff, the tails kept getting in the way of the operation, cats were much better, didn't have the problem with the tails. Mary studies her wine glass and wishes it wasn't empty. Mary tells herself Michael is a kind caring doctor, maybe he has a cat at home, she could imagine him, relaxing, after dinner, with the cat on his knee, scratching it under its chin.

. . . *it's small and furry and cuddly*
. . . *it's a torture chamber*
. . . *how can you like men? Still you continue to believe it can be done*

Mary looks at Michael. At his craggy good looks, he'd fit perfectly on the cover of a Mills & Boon. A Mr Rochester. In a white coat.

Gary brings her back, he's still talking good and evil with Jonathan, saying it's incredible what some men are capable of, he tells a story about a patient, a middle-aged woman with cancer, she'd had chemotherapy and of course got quite sick with that so she was sent home from the hospital for the weekend for a little TLC. On the Sunday afternoon the woman's sister rang the ward, very distressed, could her sister be re-admitted? It seemed her husband just flipped, who knows, maybe the shock of her dying, or the hair falling out with the treatment, anyway, over the few hours she'd been home he raped her, repeatedly, over and over, she was helpless, they've got a court order against him now.

. . . *suddenly he turned into a monster*

. . . if not all men, at least two, at least one, you continue to believe

Now Gary's wife is talking about how it feels to be a patient at National Women's after all those years of working at the hospital as a nurse. Mary says she didn't realize Gary's wife was pregnant. Mary feels a sudden tightness in her throat. Mary has been a patient at National Women's, too, but for another reason. Mary's husband Don is asking who read the paper this evening, did you read about the National Women's Inquiry, how it had been admitted that as part of student's training women are given vaginal examinations under anaesthetic without their consent, Michael says how could they be so stupid as to come right out and admit it like that, they were sure to be crucified in the media and Mary thinks, how extraordinary that we're all sitting here calmly talking like this, and I wonder how many women read that item in the paper tonight, or maybe heard it on the radio while they were in the kitchen and wondered, was it me, was I one of them, as I was laid out there, at their mercy the quality of mercy with my feet in those awful stirrups did they have a poke at me, and how many of them, and Mary begins to talk she finds herself talking about this book she's been reading, it's on this course she's been doing at the Continuing Education Department of the university, this book, it's written by a woman, a theologian, called Mary Daly, she's one of the North American Women Writers, on this course, the book's called *Gyn/Ecology*, she sets out the chapters in the following linear progression: Indian Suttee, Chinese Footbinding, African Clitoral Excision and Mutilation, European Witchburning, American Gynecology. Again, everyone laughs. Mary is a funny girl.

And suddenly she remembers, Mary Daly's chapter on American gynecology, it opens with some quotations, something about the Andes survivors, boys with violent instincts choosing both rugby and surgery, and a bit written by a woman she'd never heard of, called Charlotte Perkins Gilman:

> '. . . *my husband is a physician and perhaps – (I would not say this to a living soul, of course, but this is dead paper and a great relief to my mind) – perhaps that is one reason I do not get well faster . . .*'

When Mary had sat opposite to the gynecologist at National Women's Hospital, after the exploratory operation, she had sat there that afternoon hearing him tell her that, due to the Dalkon Shield he had put in years ago, there must have been some infection, he drew a little diagram, he didn't mind spending the time with her, he was a friend of her husband's, showing her how the egg started on its lonely journey every month but that in her case there was a blockage, in the tube, the door was locked, there was nowhere for it to go, nowhere –

> *. . . Lizzie Borden's home was 'full of locked doors that open into other rooms with other locked doors'*
> *. . . Lizzie Borden's days 'open their cramped spaces into other cramped spaces and never anything to look forward to, nothing'*

Dr Fraser, and his wife, drove Dr Crawford, and his wife, back across the harbour bridge to their hotel. It had stopped raining. 'Where do you get your sheep?' asks Dr Fraser of Dr Crawford. 'I didn't think there were any sheep in Winnipeg.' 'No, there aren't many, we get them in from the south.' 'Do you use them, for research?' asks Mrs Fraser. 'Mary is an anti-vivisectionist,' says her husband. She's feeling decidedly queasy, the lamb she'd had for dinner is sitting squat in her stomach, she can't say, it must be past midnight, she must get away or turn into a – Portia, oh Portia, how shall we ever save ourselves, and the quality of mercy, the quality of mercy but the headlights the glittering headlights, through the water streaming down from her eyes the glitter of the oncoming headlights will soon be all she can see . . .

Mary is a funny girl
Mary is a bit of a feminist
Mary is an anti-vivisectionist
Mary is a depressive but the drugs help
Mary finds herself for no logical reason wasting a sunny afternoon, achieving nothing, with the horizontal of the oak branch a lengthening shadow and her hands busy twisting the leftover strip of curtain fabric, and of course the dream makes perfect sense to me now, I've found myself here, as you have found me here, the end of the road, the house is a mess, the day gone, wasted – I would not say this to a living soul but this is dead paper – and in my hands a twisted rope, the candy-striped chintz but is desperate too strong a word with the oak branch a gibbet, around my neck a noose and no way out, you must understand that, no way out at all.

FRAN MARNO

Blood

Clarence bled for nineteen years. She put on a new pink satin sanitary belt and pinned the pad in place when she was fifteen. She pulled out her last tampon when she was thirty-four. That was seven years ago.

Clarence is forty-one. She wants to write about blood.

'Too naive,' says Kay. Kay writes intellectual post-modernist pieces. 'Feminist deconstruction of the male language gives us a position in language. We need to create our own fictions,' she says.

Clarence tries to read Kay's fictions. She can't understand them. She wonders who can.

'Depressed women, insensitive men, birth and blood. It's all been done,' Kay says.

'I haven't done it.'

'It's therapy, personal diary discourse.' Kay tasted her own blood and shouted at men in the seventies. 'Political dynamics have changed. We don't need feminist angst any more.'

Holly is Clarence's younger daughter. 'Malcolm come over while you were out,' she says. 'He brought presents for me and Jay.'

Clarence doesn't like a forty-five-year-old friend of her ex-husband hanging around her daughters.

'He read your poster. I don't think he liked it. He said "we're not all like that",' Holly says.

Clarence has not officially met Malcolm. She's angry that he has come into her house. 'I don't want men around here,' she tells Kay.

It's what Kay used to say, but now she tells Clarence, 'Lesbian separatism is too simplistic. It leaves the central core of phallocentrism intact.'

Kay co-owns a house with a homosexual post-modernist painter who is creating gay-male fictions through visual representation. The walls of her house are covered with clever male fictions that mean nothing to Clarence.

Clarence sits at her desk and writes PROUD TO BE A WOMAN at
the top of a blank piece of paper. 'Too clichéd' she imagines Kay saying.
PROUD TO BE A WOMAN she writes all over the page. Holly comes
in. She's not supposed to interrupt, not while Clarence is writing.

'I'm hurt. I want a cuddle. I said I want a cuddle.'

Clarence doesn't want to cuddle. She wants to write, not cuddle and
make it better. She remembers what Holly told her a few weeks ago.

'Malcolm likes me sitting on his knee when I get tired at the folk
club. It's all right, his daughter's eleven too and she still sits on his knee.
We're not too old. He gives us lots of cuddles. He says that no one's
too old for cuddles. He's really nice.'

Clarence doesn't want this nice man cuddling her daughter. She tells
Anne about him. She and Anne used to share complaints about men
when they'd both left their husbands. Then Anne would have agreed
with her.

'Relax,' says Anne. 'Stop giving this guy such a hard time. I'm
beginning to feel sorry for him. He's probably genuinely fond of Holly.'

'Sure,' says Clarence, 'and I suppose he sits eleven-year-old boys on
his knee and cuddles them too.'

'I understand how you feel. I've been through the anger phase myself,
but I've done a lot of growing since then. I'm more accepting. Men
are trying to change, to get in touch with their caring, feminine natures.
We need to appreciate that.'

Clarence thinks that Malcolm fancies her older daughter Holly. She
saw him from a distance yesterday at the folksingers' gathering. He
was leaning all over her, laughing, teasing, pinching her cheek and
touching her shoulder.

'Dirty old man,' Clarence blurts out.

'You're over-reacting,' says Anne. 'You'll never get beyond feminist
rage if you can't learn to trust your brothers.' Anne has a teenage son
and no daughters.

Clarence is unfashionable. She wants to complain about men and
write about blood.

Clarence was fifteen when she started to bleed.

'You're a late starter Clarie, like your mother,' her Nan told her.

'Clarie's got her period,' her Nan told Aunt Alice and Great Aunt
Jo. They sat around the kitchen table and talked about knitting patterns
and recipes and Jessie Brown who had an abortion and Elsie Davidson
who hung stained sanitary towels on her line every month.

'She never washed the blood out properly,' Aunt Alice told Clarie. 'She pegged them out where everyone could see them,' Nan added. 'Bold as brass that one,' said Aunt Alice.

Nan was glad that Clarie used modern pads. She wrapped them in newspaper and Nan burnt them in the old copper fire. 'We wouldn't want your grandfather seeing them, would we Clarie?' she'd say, poking them into the flames. Carie liked the smell of burning blood. She liked to think of her bloody pads helping to heat the washing water. She didn't like the way her grandfather had started to look at her breasts. She was glad that her school bloomers were navy blue and didn't show the stains when they were hung out to dry.

Jay is nearly fourteen and Clarence marks her daughter's first bleeding on the calendar. She writes TODAY JAY BECOMES A WOMAN in her diary and likes the formality of her statement. She buys a crystal for Jay and tells the woman 'my daughter's begun to bleed'. The woman is unimpressed. 'Bit different these days,' she says, wrapping the crystal irreverently in a kitchen paper towel. 'Nothing for us to celebrate was there.'

Clarence smiles apologetically and puts the crystal in its paper towel carefully into her shopping bag. She goes to the chemist shop and buys a pack of twenty regular Stayfree adhesive pads, and because they're in a plastic see-through carrier bag she pushes them deep down next to the crystal where no one will see them.

Clarence doesn't tell Anne that she's trying to write. Anne wins competitions with her stories and publishers are beginning to notice her. Her latest one is about two men and a woman on a skiing holiday together and Clarence finds it depressing. It's not obscure and academic like Kay's, but it's coolly objective. The woman is self-contained and remote. The story is really about the men.

'Your story's about men. They're the heroes. It's not even remotely feminist,' Clarence complains. She's disappointed. Anne used to write about women.

'It's post-feminist,' Anne tells her. 'The woman doesn't need to be central any more.'

Clarence wants to be central and she wants her daughters to be central too. She isn't ready for post-feminism. Maybe she'll grow into it. She doesn't think she wants to. She's preoccupied with femaleness and she still says rude things about the new breed of sensitive, aware men.

Clarence stopped bleeding when she was thirty-four. She pulled out her last tampon a week before she went into hospital.

'I've sewn you up nice and firmly,' the surgeon told her. 'Your husband will like it.'

Clarence was raw and bleeding and stitched and thought she'd never want sex again but she did her exercises every hour and firmed her vaginal muscles.

'You're shaping up beautifully.' His voice was fatherly, intimate and his fingers stung like needles way up inside her.

'Thank you,' she said, and blushed.

Her neighbour, Rose, brought her a gift. Clarence looked at the garden-picked flowers arranged around a bunch of parsley. She didn't want them. She'd told her friends not to bring her flowers. They gave her hayfever. Rose knew that. The ward was full of cellophaned flowers and visiting husbands who didn't know what to say to their wives, and wives without wombs who said their husband's weren't managing without them.

'Last time I was in here with my bladder complaint he didn't do a scrap of housework,' the angora rabbit farmer in the next bed confided to Clarence. 'Every time a bed got dirty he just moved to another one. I had to wash four lots of sheets when I got home.' The home-spun wool sped through her fingers and looped around the knitting needles. The flowers and get well cards spilled over on to the window ledges.

Rose's husband didn't bring flowers when he visited. He just sat on the chair by the bed looking out of context. He squeezed Clarence's hand and told her she looked pale. 'Bloodless,' she said, but he didn't get the joke. She knew the other women guessed that Paul wasn't her husband but they didn't say anything. Her husband brought her daughters in to see her in the evenings and he looked at all the other women, not at her. Clarence should have been pleased that Paul wanted to be with her but she was embarrassed that he held her hand in public like that.

'Did Rose bring you those flowers?' he asked. It was his garden too.

'I didn't know she was coming to see you.' He sounded irritated. He didn't like his wife having secrets. Clarence was tired of being his secret. She wished that he'd give her hand back and take the flowers away and leave her alone so that she could sleep and get better and go home.

Clarence is putting her writing into a folder marked 'personal'. Kay is subverting patriarchal definitions of menstruation with poetic-

theoretical formulations. Jay is sorting through her collection of free
sample packs to see if she'll have enough ultra-thin maxi shields to last
her through the social tonight.

Clarence gives Jay the crystal.

'Welcome to womanhood,' she says.

'It's beautiful. I love it,' Jay says.

'I wish my period would start soon.' Holly would love a crystal too.

'You reckon?' Jay says, laughing.

'What's it like?'

'Messy.'

'Does it hurt?'

'Of course not.'

'Look,' says Holly, wide-eyed. 'There's blood on your skirt.'

'Oh my God! Gross! What'll I wear tonight. I'd just die if it showed.'

'It would be so embarrassing,' Jay says, 'just *so* embarrassing.'

Clarence doesn't want Jay to be embarrassed. 'Wear your black
jeans,' she says. 'No one will see anything.'

'And black knickers,' Holly adds.

Jay goes to the phone and rings her best friend to tell her 'IT' has
come today. 'I'm so pissed off,' she says. 'I was going to wear my new
skirt tonight – you know – the one like yours. Tell you what, wear
your black jeans and I'll wear mine.'

PAULA GREEN

Now the Old Woman with the Stick Goes Clicking Past

That woman with those spiked heels scratching down over the footpath
outside my window scraping a noise trail down and over the footpath
to her car her car outside that she opens and then bangs the door and
then bangs again the door doesn't she know I have need of silence but
she calls out loudly to the child loudly loudly and the cars fill my silence
as they pass the hedge wide open windows but I want the cooling breeze
not the noise I can't stand the noise I can't bear the noise or snippets
of conversation I hear as the people pass and then it's the telephone
ringing ringing ringing it only stops when I lift it up to my ear hello
George yes it's George making noise but I am all right yes it's George
but I hang up it was today I thought of George remembered the huge
blue waves biting our heads off as we stood on the rocks the dangerous
rocks remember the signs at Castlepoint the fishermen curving lines
around into the heads of angry biting waves and George and I stood
on the dangerous rocks feeling the danger snap snapping at our heads
but I held my head firmly on as we walked around further and let the
wind whip the sand into our eyes like whipping the ice-cream of
Mr Whippy all over the road whip whip whippy but we do not like
your sickly sweet confection we laughed and we lived in each other's
pockets for eight days in a row for all I had was pockets I had not
expected to stand on dangerous rocks at the point with George I had
not expected to spend time in his pocket was not beastly pocket is car
horn beastly that sounded outside this window just when I did not
expect when I want silence but he too George too lived in my spent
time in my pocket that summer eight days that summer we lay remember
we lay on the sand letting the waves tease and cover when people walked
along not many not many people walked along we felt alone at the
beach it was eight days we had eight days now it is all we do is talk
George is always ringing me up disturbing me at my chair remember
though George remember as we lay on the beach under the tree in the
hot tent where the sun would wake us up get up stamp our bodies in

hot heat race run laugh scream down to the beach ecstasy in jump in
the water bite back cold back bite cold in back back to breakfast but
how can I remember with all this noise I need need to remember noise
this noise that screeching squeaking bicycle up and over the curb clunk
thump brakes whining shuffle whistle piss off child you disturb you
intrude upon my need of silence of remember with your noises of play
George George he we he and I caught the train back to Wellington
that day afternoon night night we had returned to Wellington I went
back to my empty house that night we had talked had talked a lot
especially on the eighth day we had talked I had told him stories of
the child then and the hedge house family the hedge house and then
we had returned to Wellington that night me to an empty house it felt
too empty people came back people filled up the empty city again noisy
city lights lights of night and neon signs and crowded pubs passing back
the jugs over head tops pass back excuse me and the band on stage
in the dim dark lit corner making conversation impossible but what
have you been doing they shouted shouted in my ear sore ear I don't
need shout it's the last thing I need not shout oh nothing much mucking
round I hear you've seen a bit of George lately which bit is bit George
have you seen George lately how is George awful music it's too hot
in here see you later later tonight yes yes noise noise now all the house
doors are slamming and banging with people returning from work
carrying shopping bags keys rattling in anticipation in pockets bang
slam door sorry it's the wind even the birds join in I don't mind the
birds and even before before I knew it the summer was over it was
all used up the summer holiday and I was standing with my toes curled
on the edge of the real world ready to dive in but I remembered forgot
remembered what they said and I dived I dived did dive head first but
my arms and legs were straight it was the only way I knew and there
was impact must be impact crash hurt pain laughter and yes surface
enjoy it enjoy it enjoy the swim I didn't think about George when I
curled my toes around the edge and dived he knocked though he
knocked at the door one day later day later that year that's when we
sat drinking tea together when we had not seen each other since the
railway station we had not argued raised voices glared or flinched from
touch we had not we had not we had had a story hedge house story
and then there was a long silence a seeming forever silence like at the
end of a book that lasted a long time but then but then it is finished
and there are no more pages and there is only silence that is the end
of the book I think we sat drinking tea sat drinking tea at the kitchen

table it hurt it hurt to look at each other we turned aside our arms accidentally touching a meshing of skin and we remembered the sand had we forgotten the sand I am not the person to scream outside the window the wide open window to quieten quiet quiet shut up just bloody well shut up all of you I am trying to remember I have this paper this folder of paper I am going to write a story a special story now I know the story hedge house story I want to write soon soon always soon not later later is when we walked down to the restaurant to the place where we ate and talked talked talked until there was nobody left and we walked back up the hill again always back up a hill in Wellington and then our mouths touched remember our mouths touching soon soon is when when we promised we would see each other not later as we sat drinking breakfast coffee and now the old woman with the stick goes clicking passed.

M.A. SOTHERAN

A Body Like That

Melanie. You are five foot two and you weigh seventy-three kilos – that was last week, anyway, when I made you get on the scales in the chemist shop in St Kilda. I was embarrassed for you, but you just laughed, and when we got down the road you talked me into buying another ice-cream. When you are undressed the rolls of fat hang down and overlap each other a little, and your soft breasts flow over your waist, which melts into your hips. Your flesh looks like white play-dough, waiting to be moulded in my hands. In bed your pliant body envelops my skinny one like a quilt, and I feel all sharp and angular lying there next to you, listening to your quiet breath.

Melanie, why do I love you, when you are such a slob? For instance, you don't wash your hair enough. It's fine and gets greasy so quickly – you ought to wash it every day. But you always have some excuse when I remind you. It looks so pretty when it's clean: black and shiny, with the fringe hanging softly over your eyes.

You can be really messy in the flat, too. You know it makes me angry when I come home from work and you haven't even washed the breakfast dishes or swept the floor. But then you start to tell me about the funny conversation you had with the old lady downstairs, or you show me a little plant you've got from somewhere for our window ledge garden, and I can't be impatient with you any more. You are always so pleased to see me, so full of happy plans, that I choke back my moans about the housework, and wonder why I am always so uptight.

'Let's go window-shopping!' you say, or 'Let's go to the beach!' So we take our towels and you get into those old shapeless blue bathers of yours, and I into my taut black ones, and off we go to the beach on a summer night. I prefer to go there in the evening myself, when there aren't many people around to stare like they do at weekends. Not that they ever seem to worry you, Melanie. You don't even cover up your bathers with a T-shirt to hide from the eyes. You walk into the water as if you owned the place, and if we want to get something from

the kiosk you always offer to go, while I flatten myself into the sand.
I wish I was like you, so carefree and innocent. I love you, Melanie.

Tonight is a warm night, and the water is rippling into the sand in
little greeny waves. Even though it has been a hot day, there aren't many
swimmers cooling off, just a few kids and their mothers and fathers,
and some isolated singles reading or just lying there. I want to choose
a place on the white sand that's away from all the others, but you have
to grab my hand and take me down to your favourite spot near the
surf clubhouse. And soon a whole lot of big tanned young men start
getting their surfskis ready to practise their paddling races, right near us.

Why, Melanie? What is that armour of certainty you wear, that
makes you so unafraid of people? Why do you unerringly choose to
be where the crowd is? You want to go into the water straight away,
but I persuade you to wait until they have pushed their bright skis into
the water, and are heading out towards the buoy, yelling at each other
as they always do.

Now we can go in unnoticed, so I hurry down and dive in at once,
surfacing to see you strolling in the shallow water, your bathers hanging
in tired wrinkles, the fat at the top of your soft thighs shaking a little
as you walk. You are smiling at a kid who is building a sandcastle,
pausing to offer him a shell. Hurry, Melanie, hurry in! The sharks are
heading for shore! You must hide, hide in the kind, forgiving water.
To my relief, you submerge just as the paddlers return to the beach,
so that all they can see are our bobbing heads. Now we must stay here,
and swim, until they have caught their breath and turned for another
onslaught on the buoy.

'Isn't the water beautiful tonight?' you say, and I agree, letting it
soothe me, laughing as you splash me gently and affectionately, as if
to say, 'There, what were you worrying about?' I swim a little, rolling
over and over, kicking lazily. Here in the sea we are anonymous, like
sea otters, water creatures in peaceful play. All we have to do now is
be careful with our timing, so that we can emerge from the water when
the surf club guys are far out by the buoy. I keep a wary eye out for
their return.

'I'm going in now,' I say, when I see that the time is right. 'Come
on, I'm getting cold.'

I stand up and head for the shallows, hurrying. But then, when I'm
almost there, I hear splashing behind me, and suddenly you hurl
yourself at my legs, bringing me down on to the sandy bottom in a
flurry, laughing as I push and struggle to escape your loving playful

arms. It's no use. You have taken me by surprise and I can't get away – for someone so unfit you have a lot of strength when you want.

'Melanie!' I shout. 'Let me go!'

But you are determined to have your game, so we wrestle desperately there in the shallow water, you giggling uncontrollably and me tight-lipped and seeing the surfskis getting closer and closer. Now they are shouting at us, and I can hear what they are saying over your puffs and splutters.

'Hey,' the leader shouts. 'You just aren't built for that!'

'Les be friends!'

'Perverts off the beach!'

'No dykes here!'

Their jeers rain on us as sharp as pebbles. Melanie, can't you hear? I tear myself from your grip, longing to drown myself in the six inches of water at my feet, but I could not hide if I were offered the ocean's depths, because now you stand up too, and when they see you revealed the yelling seems to fill the whole beach.

'It's Jaws!'

'No it's not, it's a bloody whale!'

'I'd kill myself if I had a body like that!'

'No wonder she can't get a man!'

Oh Melanie, my loving Melanie. I run up the beach and grab the big beach towel I always make you bring, and rush back to you, covering your shame and mine, as the jeering echoes in my ears. 'A body like that! I'd drown myself!'

You stand there with that black hair dripping all over the yellow towel, waiting for me to cover myself, and when I have dragged a reluctant T-shirt over my wet body, I hustle you away up the beach, turning our backs on the whistles and the cheers. You put your arm around my shoulder, and lean your head against me.

'You didn't let them spoil your swim?' you say, anxiously. 'You do want to go home now?'

Of course, I snap a bitter answer. 'How can you be so dumb?' I say. 'Haven't you got an ounce of pride in that fat body of yours?' I ask.

You just look at me, with that forgiving look I hate sometimes. Why can't you be angry, for once?

'Sticks and stones,' you say. 'Thanks for the towel.'

When we get home, we shut the door, and the world out, and while I gulp wine you cook dinner for me, chattering, into my silence, about what we will do tomorrow. You even tidy the flat a little, while I watch

TV in the half-dark, as the curtains ruffle in small warm night breezes. Later, in bed, we lie next to each other listening to strangers' voices, drifting through the open window. They can't hurt us here Melanie, we're as safe as rabbits in a hole. I hug you protectively, while your soft hand strokes my bony shoulders, gently and rhythmically, until I feel it slip away, and your breathing slow. You are right of course, Melanie; tidy flats don't matter, or bodies that people don't sneer at either. Lying here right now in the snug hollow of your unquestioning love I know that. You've got a vulnerable body and I've got a vulnerable heart but together we're strong and we'll live through more days like today. I know it. I know it.

But even so, Melanie, now you can't see me, I'm crying.

CHERIE BARFORD

Visiting the Seals

If I climb to the top of the hill and look down I'll find seals sunbathing beside rock-pools. They have eyes like children begging for ice-cream when their jandals are melting in tar.

The hill can be reached when the tide's low. I climb it when my desire to view seals is stronger than my fear of flax. Flax. That wind-blown, sometimes flowering silhouette in postcards. And in the distance, always the sea.

Sometimes I forget I'm an islander. A brief stroll. The taste of salt. I remember. Now, before the tide turns, I'll scale the hill's rocky feet. Pull myself through soft, gold tussock. Climb through flax.

To calm myself I've pocketed cymbals. Finger cymbals that I attach with black elastic, one to my thumb, one to my middle finger on the left hand. When I'm breathless I clip them together. Ring-g-g-g-g-g. A delicate brass reverberation that slowly fades. Settles me down.

At the top of the hill there's a Norfolk pine. I'll climb towards it. But seven steps into the flax – I'm lost. The sky has disappeared. I can't see the pine. There's only flax whipped up by the wind. It pulls me down.

Stumbling uphill towards the unseen pine, something hits my face. It's a weka. A squat, brown bird, fuming and flightless at my intrusion. I apologize. Find an avenue where flax grows in lines either side of a ridge. Follow it to the end. Sit down with my cymbals. Ring-g-g-g-g. Ring-g-g-g-g. Feeling quieter now. Breathing steadily.

I'm susceptible to colours. Avoid people wearing brown. Such a pedestrian colour. It wears me out. I bought the cymbals because their sound matched the lilac of my favourite shirt . . .

I've always loved purple. As a child I closed my eyes, lifted them to the sun and pressed the lids gently with my thumbs until the world flushed lilac, mauve, gentian-violet. And that's how I was. Always falling over. Gentian violet on my knees and on my arms where school sores festered.

I like my purple world. Purple-people survive. My Aunt Violet's twin died, but she's still alive. Her world is purple. I know this because I have her eyes. Azure. Vulnerable. Round.

Soon the tide will turn. Fishermen will row past the hill on their way to the harbour. It will be an island. The seals will be gone. Someone will stop, pick me up, crack a joke about mermaid hitch-hikers.

The flax is thinning. I'm sure the pine is near. Beyond it is a ledge sheltering the rock-pools where the seals lay. Left foot in front. Lean forward. Grab a handful of flax. Pull upwards, pushing with the right leg. Breathe out. Repeat.

There they are. The pups are growing. They're playing hide-and-seek. Jumping in and out of pools. Sniffing kina. Yawning in the sun. It's peaceful here. The distant town seems very small.

Once I lived in a small town. Its red earth and the blue sky above the petrol station combined to form a purple haze. I lived between the railway station and the army camp. Days, nights, dreams punctured by passing trains and bugles. Then one day I headed for the west coast. Visited the seals. Never went back.

It's almost sunset. The seals are swimming away. Perhaps I'll come back tomorrow. It depends on the weather. If it's windy the flax is too strong for me.

Those distant shapes are boats. I'll wade out to the end of the rocky outcrop. Stand in the water with my thumb out. Hitch a ride home.

SUZI POINTON

Shark Alert

She met him at a party. He took her home, and in the morning, after bacon and eggs, they got in his car and headed out towards the East Coast.

'Where are we going?' she asked him, after they had been driving for some time.

He took one hand from the steering wheel and pointed through the windscreen at the cloudless sky.

'It's a beauty day. I thought we might go to the beach.'

'Won't it be too crowded?' she inquired mildly, peering out the side window at the traffic that was banked up and snarling at the entrance to the Bondi freeway.

'Not in the waves,' he answered with authority. 'You'll find most of these suckers are scared shitless of the rip.'

And he sneered at the opposition. She looked less than convinced.

'Do you like the water?' he asked her.

'Mmmmmmmm . . .'

The lights changed. Everyone took off in a scramble of burning rubber and over-revved engines. He changed through three gears and looked down at her legs which she was holding raised above the swirling sea of soft drink bottles and chip cartons on the floor.

'You look like you could do with some sun,' he advised her.

'But I haven't got my togs,' she protested, hanging onto the seat as they made the wide sweep around the overpass. Far below her were ranged seemingly endless streets of red brick apartment buildings. He laughed and slapped the steering wheel with his hand.

'You won't need them where we're going. This is Sydney, mate. You Kiwis are a funny tribe. All you have to do at Bondi is keep your knickers on and you'll be lost in the crowd.'

He found her consternation amusing. He was still laughing to himself as they glided down the long hill and joined the slow-moving traffic cruising the Bondi waterfront. There were scores of young men who looked just like him; they shouted to each other from car to car with a convivial air of belligerent camaraderie and tooted their horns in glorious exaltation. Like predators they scanned the throngs of semi-naked pedestrians who were strolling under the tatty shop fronts with dabs of zinc cream on their noses and their bodies slick with oil and burned to a uniform amber.

There was no real hurry. It was a listless procession, feet slapping in rubber thongs, eyes screwed up against the glare, and cracked lips parted in slow smiles of stupefied bliss. In their arms they carried all the paraphernalia of their pleasure: bright beach bags stuffed with soggy towels and bathing trunks, eskies stacked with beer cans in a cradle of ice, ghetto blasters, goggles, lotions and sand-spattered surf boards.

She noticed that he appeared to be quite at home. He crowed with pleasure, leaning out of the driver's window to trade insults with his mates. In the parking lot he trailed one arm out the side as he howled at a group of young girls sprawled across a customized panel van. They gave him the fingers, but he pulled to a stop right next to them, with the front tyres nudging up to the edge of the crumbling sea wall.

'Here we are,' he said.

She opened the door and a searing blast of air hit her. She uncurled stiffly out of the car and winced as her bare feet made contact with the burning cement.

'You pads aren't seasoned,' he told her. 'You should go without shoes all the time and by the end of the summer you could walk across hot coals and you wouldn't notice.'

The young girls stared with narrowed eyes as she hobbled over to the edge of the wall and stood confronting the drop to the sand. From the open doors of the van she could hear the distorted anthem they were broadcasting to the passersby: 'Nothing much happening in my life . . .'

She hesitated.

'Here. I'll give you a hand.'

He was over the wall in one bound, still carrying the towels, the eskie and the transistor, and she saw how lightly he landed so that he hardly disturbed the supine couple only inches from his feet.

'Don't worry. I've got you.'

She wobbled for a moment, holding her breath, and then fell so heavily that he lost his balance and they both crashed down together on the sand. The couple next to them were showered with a fine blanket of sand but the event did not appear to penetrate their consciousness.

'Where would you like to sit?'

She scanned the crowded beach through half-closed eyes. The light reflected off the sand was so bright that she could hardly see a thing.

'What about over there?' she suggested, indicating the least congested spot.

'That's no good. That's the sewage outlet. I'll tell you what – right here'll do.'

She saw that someone had painted on the wall behind them *Be A Jerk: Go To Work*. He positioned the towel with a professional's care. 'You'll get more reflection off the concrete if you lie back this way. Wait a minute, though. I'll just get rid of that dogshit.'

She stood back while he, like a cavalier, kicked sand over the offending object. She sat on the towel at the angle he had indicated and rubbed plaintively at the singed soles of her feet. The sun beat down. She squinted at the sea which was flashing and throbbing with what seemed an alarming intensity. He squinted at the sea and waved wildly to some spindly figures in the distance.

'Wanna meet my mates?'

'In a minute . . .'

'Wanna beer?'

'No thanks.'

He dropped down and grinned at her like a young dog that wanted to play. She rummaged through her bag for her sunglasses and he dug a hole and sprawled on his back at her side.

'First we'll get up a good sweat and then we'll go for a dip, okay?'

'Okay.'

It was hard to relax. She closed her eyes but she felt the sun trying to burn through the lids like a laser beam. Behind her the traffic hissed and snarled along the esplanade. Every now and then there was a wild rebel yell emanating from the garden bar of the Bondi Tram. Above them the panel van repeated its message '. . . nothing much happening in my life . . .'

She sat up. He appeared to be sleeping. She looked further down the beach where a migrant family were setting up a picnic. For a while she watched as the mother supervised the distribution of an enormous quantity of food. A baby was playing with a half-buried beer can. Still further down on the hard strip large Amazonian girls paraded sullenly under the scrutiny of the loitering men. Behind her, ranged out along the safety railing that bordered the cliff, she saw elderly European men dressed in suits training binoculars on the topless sunbathers, sprawled below them on the sand. Finally, out beyond the first angry barrier of surf the young men in black rubber congregated like a separate amphibian tribe. They straddled their boards, riding the swell, and staring hopefully out to sea.

Beside her the young man lay as if he was dead. He wore only a pair of brief Speedos that were made out of some glittering synthetic. The rest of his body was singularly hard, lean and brown. A real physical type, she thought, looking down at her own pale legs sticking out from her skirt. She crumpled a discarded cellophane bag between her toes and wondered when the next bus might be leaving for the city.

'Hey, what are yer still doing with your gear on?'

He had opened his eyes and was sitting up, staring at her accusingly.

'Here, I'll give you a hand . . .'

Before she knew it she was stripped down to her lace bikini pants. He stared dispassionately at her pale flesh and reached into his bag for a bottle of Hawaiian Tropic.

'You're liable to get cancer with a skin like that,' he warned her, sitting beside her with one leg on either side to prevent her escape. She blushed as he smeared the oily stuff all over her, even though his hands were quite innocent and his face screwed up in a frown of concern.

'I don't think I've ever seen somebody so white in my life. Don't you lot ever get any sun over there?' he said, dabbing a large blob of zinc on to her nose.

'It's my Irish blood,' she explained. 'We don't tan, we just burn . . .'

'Well, what do you do in the summer then?' he asked her, amazed.

'I work,' she said defensively, shaking off sand.

'You can't work all the time . . .'

'I go to movies. I read . . .'

'That's the trouble with you,' he concluded triumphantly. 'You're not getting enough sun.'

He tore the tab off a can of cold beer and she watched as the foam seeped into the sand. It was gone in an instant. He belched.

'In the summer, for instance, I try to put in three or four hours a day here at least. I can't stand being indoors unless I'm seriously drinking.'

'Don't you work?' she asked him.

'Yes, of course. I hump crates in a pub four nights a week. You should get yourself a night job. That way you'd have more time free for the beach.'

'But I'm saving to go to Europe,' she protested. 'I work for a travel agency. That way you can get cheap flights.'

'What the hell do you want to go there for?' he asked her incredulously. 'The Poms are a miserable lot.'

'My ancestors came from Ireland,' she explained. 'I want to see the town I come from . . .'

'So what? Mine came from there too, but they had to come over here to learn how to enjoy themselves . . .'

'Don't you want to travel?'

'Oh, yeah.' He shrugged and dug a channel in the sand with a discarded ice-block stick. 'I was gonna split with my mate when he went to Bali but I didn't get the bread in time. He came back and said the waves were much better here by a long shot . . .'

'Aren't you curious to learn about other cultures?'

He laughed.

'What do you mean? We've got the whole bloody lot clamouring to get over here. It's getting hard enough to make yerself understand at the corner milk bar . . .'

He jumped to his feet and grabbed her by the hand.

'Come on,' he said. 'You're getting too bloody serious. Tell you what, I'll race you down to the water . . .'

They were half-way down the beach before she remembered that she was almost naked. She dug her toes in and looked back over her shoulder to where her clothes were lying crumpled on the sand.

'You step on some glass?'

'No, I have to go back and get my T-shirt . . .'

'What's the use. It'll only get wet . . .'

And he picked her up in his arms and carried her struggling through the bemused onlookers. If I kick and scream, she thought, I'll only draw more attention to myself. So she went limp and he carried her into the churning froth, where he swung her in an arc around his head.

'One, two, three . . .'

'No, no please, I've got my lenses in . . .'

'Only joking,' he grinned, setting her feet-first down in the tide.

While she staggered, trying to get her balance he was gone, plunging into the surf in a perfect sickle shape. She was stranded among the barking dogs and shrieking children. She saw him emerge, on the other side of the first angry surf break, and he waved back at her, screaming out above the thundering roar: 'Get yer hair wet!'

Then he was gone again. The whole sea bed seemed to be shifting beneath her and she dug in her toes as the water broiled and surged, being drawn in and pulled back both at the same time by two equal opposing forces. People were gambolling in the shallows, bouncing young children up and down and splashing each other with excited screams. Dogs fetched sticks. She lurched to avoid a blind bodysurfer who came from nowhere, grappling through the surf with his arms outstretched. She turned back to the beach for reassurance but now it looked as though everybody was staring at her. She crossed her arms protectively across her chest. Nothing else for it, she told herself, closing her eyes and taking a breath. Here goes, and she threw herself into the water.

At first it was a relief, going down, just to escape the glare and the noise and to feel the cool soothing water streaming over her bare skin. No pressure. She uncurled and let herself be carried up, opening her eyes to see the sun-streaked aqua patterns just underneath the surface. Coming up. But then the rip caught her, picking her up without ceremony among a tangle of other arms and legs, like a giant fisherman hauling in a net it drew everything out to sea. Struggling helplessly she was carried for some time until it evened out and she saw that she was in a calm place from which she could still see the beach and the other swimmers; it was just that everything seemed to be terribly far away. She started to swim back, just above the waterline, and watched the skyline of Bondi bob reassuringly in and out of her vision. Everything is all right, she told herself, he'll come looking for me, and if I don't panic I might even make it back by myself.

Then another swell hit her, mocking her pitiful efforts to save herself, and dragged her screaming back out to sea, although her voice was lost in the crash and boom of the tide. She took in water, and started to thresh about, shouting and beating the waves with her fists in her fury even as she went down.

It was foolish to fight, she could see that, as she went down for the last time with the water flooding into her mouth. Much better, she decided, to stop struggling and let the sea take her. There must be some purpose behind such a wilful seduction. The water was pleasantly warm, and held her gently. Out here past the breakers the rise and fall of the swell became not aggressive, but sensual. She was a mermaid, loose-limbed and naked, drifting on the current, languishing in the ardent embrace of the ocean.

But strong hands plucked her from the tide. She heard rude voices shouting to each other above the water as she was lifted up and thrown down on to a cold slippery surface. She opened her eyes and saw that she was spread-eagled on a surfboard, held in place by rough hands that gripped her limbs. Close to her head on either side were men with red screwed-up faces, eyes narrowed under the frame of their swimming caps, snorting like dragons as they drove through the breakers, their eyes firmly fixed on the shore.

She tried to tell them, no, no, I don't want to go back, leave me here where I feel happy and free, but there was water in her lungs and when she struggled they only gripped her more firmly and ignored her feeble pleas. They reached the shore and when their flailing feet touched hard ground they stood up in unison, foam streaming from them as they wrestled her board on to their shoulders and ran through the crowd.

Sullen and defeated she lay draped across the board, her limbs dangling as they bore her past the stares of the curious bystanders. When they reached the hard sand they laid her down and one of them emptied her lungs while the others stood around her in a circle so that looking up she saw only a forest of brown and hairy muscled legs. She spat in the sand.

'Where the hell did you get to?'

It was her companion from the night before. She smiled weakly and staggered to her feet. A crowd of people stood and stared. They all seemed to be looking at her accusingly. She covered her chest with her hands.

'I got caught in the rip,' she told them. They drifted away.

His face was red as he thanked her rescuers. She was not sure if it was from rage or embarrassment. He led her up the beach, and when she had sunk on to his beach towel he remained standing, looking down at her with a betrayed expression on his face.

'You're a bit of a dead loss,' he said to her. 'You should have told me you couldn't swim.'

'I can dog-paddle,' she prótested, pulling on her skirt and T-shirt. He hovered above her, looking back anxiously at the tide.

'I warned you about the rip. Bondi surf's not for amateurs. You should have stayed between the flags . . .'

She found a small mirror in her handbag and brushed off the sand to see her face, which was flushed. What a shame, she thought. More freckles. He jumped from one foot to the other, and waved to someone on the shore.

'Do you want me to drive you home?'

'No, I'm fine. I'll just sit here a minute and then I might have another go . . .'

He looked relieved.

'In that case,' he said, 'I'll get back. Me mate's offered the lend of his board and the waves are only just starting to come right . . .'

'Go ahead. I'll catch up with you,' she said, and he was gone, like a dog that had just been released from its leash. She saw him run to join a small group of similar-looking youths who were clustered around a plinth of torpedo-shaped surfboards. He did not look back.

During the time she had been in the water it appeared that nothing had changed. On the sand people sat on their towels and stared blankly out to sea. In the water the bathers continued to make desperate forays into the surf and were thrown back, their arms outstretched like religious supplicants. She felt sleepy. The sun was directly overhead now, making everything difficult, making it hard for her eyes to even penetrate the haze. She remembered how easy it had been to submit to the sea and how hard she had fought the men bringing her back to the land. She had wanted to explain to her companion, if he could only understand, that it was not the rip itself that was dangerous, but rather the temptation to succumb and be drawn out of reach over the edge of that distant shimmering unknown horizon. She shivered at the memory.

She saw that the couple on her right were being slowly buried under sand drifts. They were still asleep and their oily skins were now covered by a layer of sand. She wondered if in fact they were dead, but as she watched the woman stirred, responding to an unknown impulse, and opened her eyes. She rose to her elbows and surveyed her male partner.

'Hey, mate,' she mewed in a husky voice. 'Wake up. Yer balls are hanging out.'

He grunted and threshed about with his legs before settling quickly back into his previous torpor. She leant over and tucked them back into his trunks, efficiently, without the slightest hint of sensuality.

The sun had shifted in the sky. The shadow of the sea wall had fallen across the beach towel. She shivered, and stood up, shaking the sand from her skirt. She shielded her eyes with one hand and scanned the waterline but could not distinguish him from any of the other backlit silhouettes. She climbed the sea wall, and looked back down on to the beach to where she had lain. There was only the slightest imprint of her body on his beach towel.

She walked to the bus stop where a crowd of sand-blasted adolescents were fighting without energy among themselves. The bus came and she fought for her place in the crush, finding sanctuary at last on the top step of the rear exit while all around her people wielded surfboards and shed sand on the seats.

The driver jerked the throttle.

'I'm not going anywhere until some of you bastards move right down the back . . .'

A siren sounded from the beach. Traffic stopped and in the bus the kids stopped fighting and lined the windows. She looked out and saw the bathers running desperately from the water.

'Shark alert.'

The whole beach froze in an attitude of terror. Along the water's edge the surfers stood with their boards dangling helplessly. Parents held their children in their arms and even the dogs drew back, their hackles raised in fear. The sunbathers stood up on their towels, bleary-eyed and tousled while their transistors sang blithely on. Traffic came to a halt along the esplanade and the pedestrians lined the sea wall, pointing and whispering from behind their hands. The bus driver turned off his engine. It was so quiet that for the first time she could hear the wind, a tough optimistic wind blowing in from the sea. There was no movement. The whole beach was suspended in a primitive moment of fear and awe. Only the waves continued to roll. Shark alert.

She saw a surf boat go out, bucking over the breakers, with the same men who had brought her back to shore hanging grimly on to its sides. They raced up and down in a trajectory parallel to the sand, but the ocean protected its own and in the end there was only the black shadow of the rescue helicopter, making a slow pass down the beach, to make a chilling manifestation of their fear.

She finally picked him out, standing with the others of his kind, staring out to sea. She smiled to see him spellbound and as she watched she saw him turn back, as if her thoughts had travelled and he had remembered her. He cast about, until he spotted the beach towel, and she saw his body stiffen as he realized that she had gone. He took a few steps, first back up the beach and then, turning around, he ran desperately out into the shallows, until his mates stopped him and he stood, defeated, his arms slowly raising in an unmistakable gesture of helplessness.

HEATHER McPHERSON

Are There Any More Alice B. Toklas's Out There?

*And if there were would I want one? or she, me – forty years
on in another hemisphere, and income, and apartment?*
It's seductive to think of her caring, to contemplate her embroidery
and acute keeper's-eye. Was that all she wanted, you think?
Companion, and share in the glory? To tackle the wives, to monitor
household arrangements, to always be there . . .
and those daily tears, in the beginning? happy – or terror?
embracing dreams and strangeness or relinquishing them? A sense
of a trap – or wild violets? A turn-of-the-century upbringing's fright,
a cerebral overwhelm, a pent-spill of social uproot – or sensuous
reaches, their excitement, and encroachment, a bodyful outflow? A
glimpse of a lightless hole outside the day or the radiant day in a lit-up
bowl, or a spread-out continent . . . or, those tears, all these?
  But all she said was she'd never been loved before . . . and no woman
so loved in literature, so singularly, literally, loved, over so many years.
No frontispiece dedication and after, forgot . . . but homages,
speakings, centralities. No one-poem shrine, no set-piece embalming,
no coroner's court and thrown to the wolves, Freudians, wood-heap
. . . but jokey not-too-obscure digressions and recallings and pet names,
in odd new chants and cool-puzzle repetitions and complications and
substrata, in gusty delight and throaty ho-hos . . . and a code.
  To celebrate, cerebrate what had been before – but new, by a woman
given her head and a live-in angel, an angel who doubled, who did
transformings – to lover, soother, friend, typist, stimulant, secretary,
focus, and plain edition publisher paying the bills with pictures, and
a buffer – for a poet given belief and collaborative acts and a night-
time space to record the unrecorded, the unrecordable, to make genius,
wif-woman and wif-woman, the unacknowledged marriage, all
impediment outside.
  But movement, minds and bodies unimpeded, inside.
      *if no more Alice Bs, lots of unacknowledged movement, and
      a fantasy, forty years on in another hemisphere and apartment.*

PHILIPPA MANSFIELD

Lullaby

Two under two – what hell.

Oh, don't get me wrong: we used modern science all right. I posted pills down my throat with the optimism of a kid posting twenty cents into space invaders but in my case –

'You're one of the unlucky ones,' the doctor said. At that stage, abortion was illegal.

'Never mind,' I said, 'We'll cope.'

And we did.

Which was just as well because for my friend Althea it wasn't quite the same – not all cuddles and fluffy nappies and candy-smelling baby-powder. Or if it was at the beginning by the time they got to the ages of three and four . . .

If you were around then you probably read about it in the paper. 'Modern-day Medea' some smart-arse wrote. What would he know about it, grubbing all day for a 'good' story, getting a fat cheque at the end of it? What would he know about people's motives, about women like Althea and me?

I guess, if I'm honest, I was just lucky. The times I felt like beating my kids to pulp I'd lock them in their rooms so they couldn't hurt themselves and I'd go for a walk outside. Or I'd put on earphones so I couldn't hear them screaming and when I calmed down go back and be really nice.

If only I was deaf, I used to think, I'd be a happy mum. Because, believe me, that screaming like a circular saw, going on and on and on in your brain, can slice it to little bits.

Althea said it never affected her like that, even though she was looking a bit run down. But weren't we all? It was different from now, believe me.

Women's liberation had hardly begun. Husbands earned the money and came home to a clean house, clean children and a meal. They said. 'What've you been doing with yourself all day?' but didn't want an answer – it was all so boring. Besides, with a washing machine and a vacuum cleaner who could complain about working hard?

They didn't understand the worries you had with kids hurting themselves and being ill, the feeling you got sometimes that you might be the one to do the hurting. There weren't any of those support groups then. You'd had kids so you must love them, it was as simple as that.

I think I did begin to get a bit alarmed about Althea the day she kept Brett and Sheree off kindergarten and came to visit for lunch and quoted the Bible at me all the time, but I didn't think it was anything serious.

She'd been religious as a girl, well so had I for a time, but I'd given it away for boys. She had a belt with her. She took it out of her bag and laid it on the table and said very calmly, blankly even:

'You just watch it, Brett, or you'll get a taste of this. Spare the rod and spoil the child.'

Brett, who was a stocky, fair-haired little boy, a real terror, into everything and cheeky too but cute all the same, stuck his tongue out and went 'wa-wa-wa'. After he'd run off Althea said:

'I worry about him, y'know? He won't do a thing I say. What'll I do when he's older? He'll get into trouble I know.'

I just said, 'You worry too much Al. All boys are like that. He'll grow out of it. You should see Jason at times. He's a proper little sod.'

We talked about this and that – although when I look back I seem to have done most of the talking – they stayed for lunch, we took the kids for a walk to the park, and around two the three of them left.

'He'll be at school in a year, Al,' I said as we climbed the path. Brett was shrieking 'Bang! Bang!' and pulling the heads off the daisies. 'Six months, that's all, and after that it'll be Sheree's turn. You won't know yourself.'

But Althea just sighed. She didn't say anything.

I suppose I should have seen the warning signs but you don't unless you're looking for them.

Anyway, I didn't see Althea again for the rest of the week. To tell the truth I was so busy that it wasn't until the Friday night that she even crossed my mind. I'll ring her tomorrow, I thought, as I was bathing the kids all ready for Bruce to come home with the takeaways. I turned on the TV for the six o'clock news and had just sat down hollering at the kids who were both trying to climb on to my lap at the same time to get dried when a picture of Althea's street, two ambulances and a couple of police cars flashed on to the screen. It took me a second or two to realize they were stopped right outside Althea's place. Just then a well-dressed guy with a mike stepped forward and started to speak.

I can't remember exactly what he said – it's sixteen years ago now, you don't remember things like that – but a few phrases like 'appalling tragedy' and 'Mrs Bracy seemed perfectly normal to the neighbours' sunk in and I began to get the picture that something terrible had happened to Al.

He kept on and on and I just sat there stunned, as cold inside as if I'd swallowed an entire packet of frozen peas, thinking, What the hell've you done, Althea? What the hell've you done? over and over to myself. I didn't even notice the kids fighting, just prayed, Oh God, please let it be all right, please, please, and the guy went on talking, saying they had taken Althea to hospital but there was no hope for the children, and I couldn't even cry, thinking of Brettie's cheeky, bright little face, Sheree's pigtails which were about an inch long to keep the hair out of her eyes.

When Bruce came in I was still sitting there. For some reason the kids had quietened down. Sometimes I think they're like animals: they know when you're really sad. I said Althea was in some kind of trouble and that I wanted to go over to her place and help so he'd have to look after the kids. He didn't look exactly chuffed but he agreed provided I wasn't too long.

'Just don't prang the car,' he added. I thought at the time this was unnecessary, but actually he was right.

I trembled all the way out to Althea's on the motorway. I suppose, really, I shouldn't have been driving but at least it stopped me thinking. One of the worst things about moving to the city for work was ending up so far away from one another. This was why Al and I had lost touch a bit. You couldn't just jump on a bicycle as we used to in the country, and unless Tom was sick he wouldn't let Althea have their car. This meant she was pretty well stuck at home. You sure as hell don't want to go lugging two babies around on a bus if you can possibly avoid it. It takes the fun out of living.

I got to Althea's street sooner than I'd expected and sat for a minute or two with the motor running wondering what I should do. I suppose I had some silly idea that Brett and Sheree might need me. I'd heard what the reporter had said but hadn't taken it in. In my mind there'd been some kind of accident and Althea had been hurt. Little did I know.

I pulled the car over and parked on the corner. Going up to a cop at the road block – a young guy – I said:

'Excuse me, I don't want to push in but I've just heard about Althea – ah – Mrs Bracy. She's a really good friend of mine. I wondered if there's anything I could do to help?'

He looked at me kind of strangely.

'Sorry. No one can go in.'

'Look, I know Althea'd want me to do what I could, honestly,' I said. My voice was a bit shaky. 'Believe me, I really am her best friend. She'd want me to help, I know.'

But he just shook his head.

I stood there dithering – I didn't feel like getting back in the car and driving home again – and then suddenly Tom came out of the house, stumbling along between two cops, his hands over his face, crying loudly, something I'd never imagined Tom doing. He was letting out great harsh tearing noises like some rusty machine which had just started up after not working for years. It was a terrible sound.

I called out, 'Tom, Tom,' and pushed past the cop and when I got close enough to him I said, 'For Christ's sake, Tom, what's happened, what's happened?' and for a moment he just stood there making this terrible noise before he took his hands away and stared at me. The edges of his skin were sharp and grey, his eyes bloodshot. He shook his head from side to side.

I'll say this for the cops – they could easily have sent me away, I suppose. I wasn't family – Althea's folks lived down country near mine – they had only my word for it that we were close friends, but I guess they could see Tom was glad I was there.

He started speaking in a croaky voice, his speech slurred as if he were drunk: 'The kids – kids –' I saw then that whatever I'd been imagining was completely and utterly wrong.

I put my hand over his. His skin was hard and grainy from carpentering. I pulled his arm.

'Let's sit down somewhere.'

'Not in –' he said.

'Okay.'

We sat down on the grass verge behind a police car where the neighbours behind the barricade were out of sight. It was after eight o'clock but still quite light and warm, too early for dew. For a long time Tom didn't speak. I put my arm around his shoulder. It was a funny thing to think at a time like that but I couldn't help noticing how different he smelt from Bruce – an odour which I guessed came from working with wood, and much nicer than Bruce's smell of oil and grease. I read in a magazine once how the wives of mechanics get cancer more than other women. It bothered me at the time, but what else could Bruce do? Besides, he's been a good father.

At last Tom began to talk. Staring in front of him he told me what had happened in a way which reminded me of the Christmas Play at Jason's kindy where the kids speak slowly, carefully, trying to remember what they've been told to say.

After a time he stopped crying and a cop asked if he could go with them to the police station. I offered him to come back to our place when he'd finished but he said he'd rather be on his own. I drove back home in a state of shock. I couldn't even tell Bruce for an hour or so and when I'd finished he looked at me and I knew he was wondering if I could ever do the same.

I don't know what made me think of it again today unless it's that Brett would have been twenty in a few weeks. Jason and he shared the same birthday. I used to be pretty regular at first but I don't go and visit Althea as much now as I used to; it just upsets me. She's either in one of her 'good' patches and remembers what they've told her she did and cries, or they've had to give her more pills because she can't stand it and she sits like a zombie, her face all puffed and grey.

The doctors say unless there's a miracle she'll never come out. They let her spend a weekend with Tom once but she tried to jump out of the car and the time she came to me it was sleeping pills. They say for her personal safety she's got to stay where she is though if you ask me she should be allowed to commit suicide if she wants. Althea loved those kids before she had that – fit. I can imagine what it must be like.

Sometimes when I used to take Jason to play soccer I had to pass the house. If there'd been any other way I'd have used it but the park was at the end of the road and backed on to a beach. Tom decided to go to Australia when he could see Althea wasn't going to get well. The house was put on the market but it didn't sell for a year or two even though the agent kept putting the price down. I suppose people had to forget.

I never told my two what really happened at the time, just said Althea had an accident while driving the car. They were twitchy about getting into ours for a while but it seemed better than the truth. Since then I've never brought it up.

Funny how you can't help feeling guilty, can't help thinking, If only I'd kept a better eye on her, but honestly it was hard to see, besides what could I have done?

The worse time was when I used to watch Jason and Kylie as they were growing up and wonder – could I? could that ever be me? I used to see Althea turning to her Bible for a message, the page falling open at random at Isaac, her sharpening the knife from the kitchen drawer. I saw her praying for guidance, waiting for God to stop her hand, believing, when he didn't, it was right. I'd see her running the bath, calling the kids, see the change in Brett's face, when, lured into the room behind the shut door, he knew what she was going to do. I'd hear little Sheree's scream when it was her turn, sense Althea's crazy reasoning – I'm doing this because I love them – watch the water crimsoning even deeper in the bath. I'd see my own children's legs running brown and strong in the sun and want to crush them to me, keep them safe forever. I'd wonder – and I still do – why things have to happen this way.

WENDY POND

Journal of a Hanger-On

A Birthday Party

In the late afternoon Jane Bowers cycled over to Wharf Road to rig
her sailing dinghy, but there was only a trickle of breeze in the bay
with meanders of placid water and reflections along the cliff edge.
Instead, she walked up through the pines to Millie and Kate's where
they gathered cherry plums from the tree outside the living-room
window. Jane packed a dozen plums to take to town for Gillespie's
birthday.

On her way home, she stopped at the phone box and rang Gillespie.
What was he up to? she asked. Sorting through the litter they had
collected, he said.

'Where from?'

He said they had been to Miranda to empty the pitfall traps. Had
a picnic and went to the hot springs, she thought. She pedalled on up
the hill. So that's how it is. Picnics with Crowhurst each weekend.

Jane shopped and made the trifle with peaches and cream on a jelly
base. She iced the cake, placing it in the middle of the table with the
cherry plums around it, and was looking out the kitchen window when
Gillespie drove up the drive. He sat for a while in the car, reading,
and then slowly got out and unloaded the boot without looking up.

'Happy birthday!'

'Is there time for a jog before tea?' he asked.

'It's a very lovely evening. Drive to the park and I'll come with you.'

'Oh. Oh well, all right then,' he said.

The trees stood widely spaced, lofty, European. Jane slipped through
the strands of number-eight wire, circling the hill to reach the summit.
She saw the western suburbs concealed in haze, locked in the vision
imported by nineteenth-century painters. Tiny figures of joggers bobbed
along the stone-walled drives.

In the north-east, the hill's shadow stretched across the greensward of the archery range, through the line of lombardy poplars, and on into the houses and streets. She imagined the birthday tea. Gillespie, Crowhurst and herself sitting at the table round the cake with the cherry plums, and the raspberry jelly at the bottom of the glass bowl glowing in the late afternoon light.

Gillespie was waiting at the car, damp from his run. His towelling hat shortened his forehead, erasing the aura of a scientist. Jane turned towards him in her bucket seat.

'Through friendships we open new vistas,' she said. 'I grew up on stories of foxes and rabbits. Your knowledge of native insects reveals a hidden fauna. Gillespie, why haven't you invited me to join your expedition?'

'Because you're not a naturalist. You wouldn't have anything to do.'

'Why not invite me for my sake, for the landscapes I could paint?'

'I don't know. It just didn't crop up. You can come if you want to,' he said.

At Frankton Airport they stood on the tarmac like early aviators. Rita Angus hung around them, in the slant of the slopes, the yellow, the blue. The great adventure was afoot.

'Gillespie,' she said, 'you would have left me out.'

The leading protagonists of this journal are Terrence Gillespie, Fellow of the NZ Entomological Society, Dr Henry Crowhurst of Carnegie Institute, and the artist, Jane Bowers.

Gillespie's Nightmare

The Remarkables, the Remarkables, so blue, so black, so stark. The shout of triumph, the gasp of sharp air. From Queenstown they drove through Arcadia to Paradise and entered the red beech forest. They spread their parkas on the picnic bench and ate their packed lunch. She was there beside the open boot in her red sandshoes and navy boilersuit. She was there at the foot of the waterfall, where the water dashed on the mossed ledges and dripped from the mossed clefts. She was there by the rotted log where they lifted the mossed bark and shook the crushed wood through their canvas sieves. She stood in the crowd of sandflies and laughed as they scowled and swatted their tender skin, those two entomologists in mental disorder from the naonao, the naonao, the little black blighters, the sharp biters, the shout of outrage, the welds on their fair skin, at Paradise.

Gillespie came back to the car with his heavy canvas sieve and bags of debris. It was drizzling. He stood by the boot, placidly wiping his glasses with his handkerchief.

'We'll pick up Crowhurst down the road.'

'Give me the keys, I'll drive.'

'It's all right, thanks,'

'Oh, but I'd like to.'

'You're not an official member of the party.'

Oh! the splash of water on the mossed cleft.

Oh! the slam of a car door.

Late into the night Crowhurst sat working at the microscope with a bare bulb lighting the tray of insects. He worked with both hands, moving the tray with one and holding the tweezers in the other, sorting the insects with mechanical manoeuvres. Dreaming, Jane was woken by a yowl from Gillespie. Crowhurst was standing stock still in front of the table, his skin sallow, his hair lank, a northern raider. Gillespie was sitting up in bed.

'I was having a nightmare,' he said. 'Pursued by wild cattle. A beast charged me.'

They established that as Crowhurst rose from the microscope, he had stepped in front of the bare bulb and cast his shadow across Gillespie.

The yowl of fear, the heart's leap.

Jane's Oversight

In the morning, Jane got up and made three lunches. Then she cooked three breakfasts, cleared the table, washed and dried the dishes, cleaned her teeth, packed her bags, put on her tweed jacket and walked into town to get the grocery order. The Remarkables were bitumen blue.

They set out for Makarora. From the back seat Jane saw that they crossed the Crown range. At the brow, the naturalists stopped to beat the native broom and gather tussock litter, while Jane sketched in the sun, in the crotch of those yellow hills. She watched them move across the hill face: Crowhurst in a short-sleeved shirt and straw hat, purveying his imported vision, and Gillespie winding along a sheep track, unaware of her perspective.

In the Cardrona Valley they caught up to a herd of Hereford cattle. Horned cows with calves at a loitering pace, three men with sticks and a pack of dogs. On the river flat they stopped for lunch. By the viper's buglos, by the roadside broom, Jane laid out her parka and opened her paper bag. By the yellow hawkbit, by the roadside tarragon, Gillespie heard the cattle mooing. Jane closed her sketch book, she snatched up the lunch bags, she grabbed her shoes.

They drove to Lake Wanaka, to the grassed banks and the picnic seats and swings, to the poplars and willows that grace our lakes' edges. At Hamilton, at Karapiro, at Taupo, at Queenstown, mown grass and willows right to the water's edge. Postcards of golden poplars, postcards of lake reflections, postcards of green swards. At Wanaka, Gillespie asked for his vials.

'I gave them to you at lunch,' he said. 'I asked you to put them in my brief case.'

'If that's what you asked me to do, then that's what I did,' Jane said. Then she recalled that at the sight of the cattle she had sped from the crushed grass, seeing herself shunted by a front runner, mooing for her lost calf.

A Debate

They drove on, along the shores of Hawea. The putrid shores, the wracked shores, the adjustable shores of Hawea.

'Crowhurst,' Jane said. 'Why did you come here? Can't New Zealand scientists do it themselves?'

'Crowhurst is a world specialist,' said Gillespie. 'He has brought new methods of collecting which add greatly to our knowledge of the fauna.'

'Do you mean New Zealanders aren't doing their job properly?'

'There aren't enough of us,' said Gillespie. 'There are ten thousand species of insects to describe.'

'But a northern hemisphere vision is holding us up. Take these forests of moths. In every New Zealander's childhood is a story of a lepidopterist with a butterfly net in the meadows, instead of a high wattage light bulb in a beech forest at night. The museums have displays of gaudy Brazilian butterflies and ignore our subtly marked moths, camouflaged to lichens and barks. Isn't it better for us to proceed ourselves, for the fauna to be observed and described with our own vision, our own sense of this country?'

Gillespie drove steadily along the loose metal road. 'We don't know yet what's in this country, and it is the scientists who are demonstrating its uniqueness in terms of world fauna. Its particular eccentricity: the number of flightless species, for instance. It's precisely the scientists who are overcoming the northern hemisphere bias.'

'Science is international,' Crowhurst confirmed. 'It has no preference to vision.'

'Just your one ubiquitous vision.'

Gillespie glanced at Jane in the rear vision mirror. 'We developed the microscope. We've looked more closely than any other culture,' he said.

Nature at Risk

At Makarora, they took a motel unit and shortly set off along a nature walk on the edge of the Mount Aspiring National Park. This walk traversed a small island of podocarp forest.

'A good track for night collecting,' said Gillespie, and they returned to the motel in the mid-afternoon.

The Memory Log of G.M. Hassing,
Sailor, Pioneer, & School Master,
died 1928.

'. . . *The Makarora valley was at that period covered by an entangled, impenetrable mass of cabbage trees, flax, and fern, growing to a height of 8ft to 10ft and the ground a jungle of dried and decayed vegetation over which it was utterly impossible to make any headway. The only access to the bush was by following the river beaches and fording the river wherever obstructions presented themselves. To get over the difficulty in our attempt to reach the bush we started a fire at the head of the lake. This soon developed into one unbroken, seething ocean of flame from hillside to hillside, and fanned by a southerly wind, it raged for three days and nights, travelling up the valley 20 miles. It was a terrific blaze, that levelled everything in its course, and disclosed the charred remains of an old Maori pa near the bush, the old Maori Kaika Paikai (the place of abundant food).*

'*This great fire transformed the appearance of the country, so that in March 1865, when the late explorer William Docherty and I started on our exploring trip by way of lake Wanaka, the Makarora valley presented a beautiful carpet of luxuriant grass, over which it was a pleasure to travel . . .*'

That night, Gillespie went back into the forest. On the outskirts, he stood listening for the hum of chafers. Then he opened out his beating tray and hit the overhead branches sharply, searching the tray in the light of his headlamp. He shook the debris off the tray, folded it up, and walked further into the forest. His headlamp picked up the shining wing-covers of tiny beetles feeding at night on the moss. It caught the spread of the canvas tray, the front of his check woollen shirt, his face lined and absorbed as he ran his beating-stick lightly down the trunks of the trees, gathering on to his tray the gallers, the strippers, the cambium borers and shoot destroyers, the diverse weevils, the byrrhid beetles, the phytophagous moss insects.

They travelled west over the Haast Pass. The grey-green forest slopes slid apart, the blue-grey river bed broadened, and they ran along fence lines of mossed posts and swampy paddocks where inroads of pasture ambled round trees and heaps of stumps. They got out at the coast and ran through the dunes to the sea. The black swells, the sinking sand, the undertows: the West Coast confronting the Tasman Sea.

From Haast they drove north through the iron-pan belt of pakihi swamp, stopping for lunch at Doughboy Creek. Crowhurst went westwards with his litter tray and cloth bags, heading for the forested dunes. Gillespie simply ducked into the trees beside the car. In the wet moss meadows of that seething forest he heard the sound of trucks along the main road, and through his sieve went the archaic *Nothoderodontus*.

A Glimmer

Their crib in the pakihi swamp had wirewove beds with candlewick bedspreads, lino floors, and batten conduits for the electric wiring. At home, they hung the extractors in the wardrobes and their damp clothes on the verandah, placed the microscope on the kitchen table, and agreed to keep the door closed on account of the naonao, the ubiquitous naonao.

In their crib in the pakihi swamp there was a large glass, a medium-sized glass, and a small orange plastic tumbler. Gillespie placed them on the kitchen table with two bottles of beer.

'Jane, do you mind,' said Gillespie, 'having the orange glass?'

'I've got the vege water to drink.' Later, Jane said, 'Gillespie, why did you offer me the plastic beaker?'

'I thought you might like the colour.'

'Why didn't you have it yourself?'

'You usually drink less than me.' Hapless, Gillespie asked, 'Is that why you didn't want any beer?'

A Search for Flightless Beetles

Travelling on, they came to the Franz Joseph glacier. Gillespie's attempt was to reach the slopes of Mount Moltke where he would search for flightless alpine beetles, isolated during the last glaciation. Crowhurst would continue to collect litter in the lowland forest. At dusk they would rendezvous in the pub.

Jane climbed with Gillespie. She caught the sweet scent of native broom in flower and glimpsed flares of red rata on the hillsides. As they came round on to the south face of the saddle, the canopy of bush gave way to tussock and the ridge rose into a white wall of vapour. Its southerly trend was consistent with the bearing of Mount Moltke, so Gillespie set out.

Clambering up and down the hummocking ridge in the course of the afternoon, he came to a cleft. In a lifting of the vapour, he faced a forested wall towering vertically above him, and a second peak rising behind. Gillespie lay back amongst the tussock in the yellow cocoon of his wet-weather gear. As he slept, orographic cloud swirled up the cleft.

Jane strolled in an alpine garden of giant buttercups and daisy heads. At hand, the silver tussock blades warped across each other and between the clumps were patches of piebald mosses. Through the drizzle the tussock gave off a vibrant mustard glow.

Plodding back, Gillespie recounted his dream. He was heading for the Mahia peninsula in the Ford Eight. Sheer walls of conglomerate rose beside and ahead of him. He reached a look-out point near the summit and got out of the car. The open ocean was slate green. Below, the sea was groaning in the rock caverns. The ferry was due to leave. He drove at speed down the hillside to the wharf. The tide was washing in around the motor spirit pumps and he had to dodge the waves to reached the ticket box. It was empty. A fisherman told him that the Cook Strait ferry had left the day before and would no longer berth at this wharf, owing to the rise in sea level. He recalled the leather suitcases strapped on to the carrier, and the labels saying 'Christchurch'.

As it turned out, the Franz Joseph settlement didn't have a pub. They picked up Crowhurst walking resolutely north along the main road through the pakihi forest. Old kahikatea stood raggedly against the orange sky.

Crowhurst Clinches the Debate

That evening, Crowhurst proceeded as he had every night, with the microscope on the kitchen table and a reading lamp directed on to the tray of insects, picking out each creature and dropping it into a vial. He had a specimen of Heterojapey, a missing link connecting earwigs to springtails. Crowhurst got up and stood aside. Gillespie, without sitting down, looked through one eyepiece of the microscope.

'Crowhurst,' Jane said, 'there are some naturalists in this country who don't want Maori names to be used in the binomial system.'

'Well, of course,' replied Crowhurst, 'scientists at Carnegie Institute, with an African name here, a Javanese name there, don't know the meaning of those names.'

'Scientists give each other's names to insects,' Jane said, 'with less meaning than a Maori name.'

Gillespie was refocusing the eyepiece. 'On the contrary, that's how we scientists record our ancestors.'

'Then who is New Zealand's fauna being classified for? World scientists or ourselves, the indigenous people?'

'You can use Maori names yourselves,' said Crowhurst.

'The categories are different. The old store-keeper at Te Puru uses papapa for things that scuttle away, like slaters and cockroaches.'

Gillespie began filling the vials, and Crowhurst returned to the microscope. 'People prefer the finer distinctions of science,' he said.

Crowhurst worked on through the night, adjusting the dish of specimens and advancing the tweezers, with the fractional pauses of a hydraulic lift changing from one position to the next.

During the course of next morning, Jane saw in the sky a thick cloud, segmented like the mouldering skin on sour milk, gaining height above the trees. The lower cloud boiling up was bruised with lime and purple: smoke from a Forest Service burn-off. Rita Angus had seen it too, and when Gillespie and Crowhurst returned at dusk they likewise stood in the yard, their gaze lifted towards the hills.

Homeward Bound

With the weeks' end, they began the homeward leg through Arthur's Pass. They took a cabin on Camping Flat, corrugated iron painted romany red. It had belonged to the railway engineer. Blue lupins were flowering around it, and through the four-light casements the beech forest towered over the roar of the river. Gillespie lit the pot-belly stove, Crowhurst hung the calico bags of litter to dry on the fire surround, and Jane made a stew which they ate on their laps.

At nightfall, she watched the sheets of rain move across the hill face, striking the green-black forest with a sharp hiss. In those landscapes, waterfalls break the cover of every valley.

Gillespie was up at seven to empty the pitfall traps. The beech forest was clean and light. He worked round to the eastern face and climbed steadily up the ridge line. Then the tide of cloud covered the pied snow peaks and he stood on his own tussock ridge, turning stones.

They drove back to Christchurch through Rita Angus country, Cass and the Craigieburn range. Jane's heart sang. How sinuously the lines portray those austere yellow hills, those blue mountains, those braided river plains.

FRANCES CHERRY

Undertow

Fingers creep across her bare flesh, touching, caressing. She moans, sighs, as if she's asleep. 'Mmmm? What?' She shuffles, moves away in exaggerated, still-asleep fashion.

Christine follows, murmurs in her ear, smoke breath wafting across her cheek. 'I love you.' *Love you love you love you . . .* echoing echoing . . .

'What?' she says, turning, knowing she has to. 'Oh . . . That's nice.' Hoping Christine doesn't ask, do you love me, too?

The hand begins to creep again, gentle, loving.

She puts her hand behind Christine's neck. Her fingers dabble, tickle, scratch at Christine's neck. Thinking, thinking. Wanting to scream and scream . . .

'Your hands are so soft,' Christine says.

'Let's have a cup of tea.' She throws the bed clothes back and jumps out of bed. Her feet pad down the long hallway, wanting to go on and on. Out the door and down the road. Running in the wind. Free. Free.

She might if she wasn't naked.

She flushes the toilet, goes into the bathroom, rushes water into the sink, looks at her face in the mirror. 'What should I do?' she asks.

In the kitchen she puts the jug on, talks to the cat and dog, collects last night's bottles, takes the over-loaded plastic rubbish bag out of the kitchen-tidy and puts it in the outside rubbish bin. She looks at the garden, inhales the morning's aromas, freesias, new-cut grass.

She pours the tea and puts it all on a tray with a bowl of sugar. She will not put the sugar into Christine's tea. She can do that herself.

Christine sits up blinking, smiling, pulling the bedcovers across her thin, almost boyish chest. She is amazed at Christine's modesty, even in front of her children she wouldn't run naked. Whereas she, especially after Brenda's wild abandoned everything-swinging-to-the-world nakedness, doesn't really worry, even if the neighbours happen to catch a glimpse of her through the windows. Funny how people are different.

'Thanks love,' Christine says, holding an arm out, 'come and have a cuddle.'

She puts the tray on the bed and sits on top of the blankets at Christine's feet. 'It's going to be a lovely day. Must get out in the garden again and make the most of it.'

'Plenty of time.'

'Hell, it's nine thirty,' she says.

'That's all right. What's the rush?'

Why can't she say, simply say to Christine, I don't want to? She takes a deep breath. 'I don't want to.'

'Oh okay, then.' Christine lifts her legs over the side of the bed. 'You should have said.' She stands, pulls her T-shirt over her head and stares through the window.

'We can still have a cup of tea, can't we?' She remembers the way Brenda would have sat there making her feel terrible.

'I'd better get going.'

'Why? You didn't want to before. You said there was all the time in the world before.' She watches Christine put her watch on. She wishes Christine would go. Why is she feeling guilty? Trying to stop her? 'Why can't I say I don't want to make love? It doesn't have to be the end of the world.'

'No.' Christine sits on the side of the bed, away from her, arms hanging between her legs, staring at the floor. 'No, it doesn't.'

'What about last night? You can't complain about that. Can you?'

'No.' Christine picks up one of her running shoes and undoes the laces. 'I can't complain. You certainly threw yourself into it.'

She stares at Christine's sharp shoulder blades, so different from the roundness of Brenda's back. 'You're making me feel bloody upset.'

'Well, why don't you tell me what you really feel? I know there's something wrong.'

She falls back on the bed. Say it, say it, a voice inside her head says. Here's your opportunity. You can't waste it. 'It's just that. Well . . . I get confused. Don't know what I feel sometimes. I'm afraid of being trapped again. You know how terrible it was with Brenda. I couldn't bear that again.' Tell her you can't stand her smoking (at least Brenda smelled nice). Go on. The smell on her breath, in her hair, in her clothes. That she has five teaspoons of sugar in her tea, doesn't know anything about nutrition. That she takes her kids to McDonald's all the time, smokes all over them.

'I do everything to suit you,' Christine says. 'I come to your place all the time. You never come to mine.'

'Well, I've still got the children to look after. You're free every second week.'

'They *are* old enough to look after themselves!'

'Richard's only fourteen. Come on.'

'How come we can go out, then? Eh?'

'You know I worry about it. I couldn't leave them all night.'

'Mmmm.'

'Don't be angry.'

'I'm not angry,' Christine sighs. 'Just sad.'

'Oh God, don't be sad.' She moves over to Christine and puts her head on her hard back.

'Look,' Christine says, not turning, 'I'll just go home. I've got things to do. You do your gardening or whatever. And we'll both have a bit of a think. Eh?'

'All right, then.' She feels her breath gliding out of her in a strange release. It will be all right. Let her go, let her go.

She follows Christine down the hallway, stands and hugs her, watches her walk up the path, close the gate and disappear.

She stands for a long time not moving, staring at the trees by the gate waving in the breeze.

And then she feels it. Small at first like a tiny sharp flame in the pit of her stomach. She puts her hand over it, willing it to disappear, almost hoping it is only her imagination but she feels it spread through her fingers and up her diaphragm so that she has to lower herself to the floor and curl up into a ball with the weight of it. Tears fall out of her eyes and on to the floor. 'Oh Brenda,' she says, 'I can't bear it, I can't let this happen again.' She crawls through the dining-room and into the hall, pulls the telephone off its table and dials Brenda's number.

ELIZABETH SMITHER

The Girl Who Loved Mathematics

She was tall and thin like the irreducible first digit, unless you reduced it to fractions, those fey incomprehensible hieroglyphics that reminded me of freckles. I was only good at language and algebra, which was mathematics disguised, letters doing the adding for numerals or concealing themselves in a brake of brackets. We had a teacher that year who didn't like Keats but it was always considered superior to be good at maths.

As for geometry, it was and has remained, as incomprehensible to me as some branches of modern art: Cezanne perhaps, leading the way with his square lightly dappled boulders and trees barely held in shape, as though they stayed that way only for human perception and might otherwise fly apart into the atoms they desired to be. Any angle formed a little tent with a guy rope and the possibility of a storm: I loved Keats but wanted the world he inhabited to be flat.

But Gilberte, I'll call her that, though it's not her real name, loved mathematics with a passion. Her father was some high official who presumably dealt with estimates and figures; it was thought she inherited her talent from him. She had three brothers with no noticeable gifts at all, except riding motorbikes and drinking, and her mother was a frail doll-like woman who seemed to hang on her husband's every word.

Gilberte was good at science too and it was she who expertly made up .1 molar solutions: tap-water first and then a pipette at the end, and understood them: the rest of the class couldn't see why we needed the pipette at all. We were obviously destined to be mothers, wiping the sides of plates clean of gravy stains while she was designed for stars and nebulae.

It was Gilberte who sensed something was wrong one day when the class was engaged in making a gas, sulphur dioxide I think it was. The teacher, who had been called away for quarter of an hour - it was safe to leave the class in Gilberte's hands and the instructions listed on the blackboard - came running up the stairs. Gilberte led us out on to the patch of grass near the Art Block where we lay on the grass for the rest of the period.

The periodic table of atoms - again I misunderstood it because my mind instantly darted into a medieval world of monastic severities and humanism, if there was such a thing in the Middle Ages. Though the atoms in their separate squares seemed severe and complete, like a chain of Carthusians, they obviously possessed the desire to join and colonize. Among these valencies and outstretched arms Gilberte moved with her own grace.

We were a motley class, except for Gilberte. It wasn't long before she outstripped her teachers, in science and maths, and there was talk of allowing her to cycle to the Boys' High School for the competition. But somehow this proposal, which might have had unforeseen benefits, was not taken up. It got so by the third term, when the teacher absented herself more and more, that Gilberte took the class. She stood on the dais and wrote the instructions for experiments on the board, each step numbered. The teacher's instructions were unfailingly vague - she had been at Cambridge as a young woman which surely promised something better than teaching us - but Gilberte wrote each minute step carefully as though we were a cooking class.

Afterwards, as we had on the day of the gas, we filed out decorously and sat in the sun. (Even on the day of the gas there had been no rush: either we had not understood the seriousness or, more likely, we were remembering *The Girls of Slender Means,* which was a class book). There was a sheltered lawn behind the old library and close to the road where none of the juniors went; though they were scornful of school it seemed they only felt safe in its centre. Whereas we, who in a few months would escape to the outside world, had instinctively chosen a place near the road.

It was sunny and quiet on the lawn and the trees were old and gnarled with soft sparse rings of grass under them. We sat on our satchels or blazers or stretched out Roman-fashion, though how the Romans ate oysters from Brittany lying on their sides was incomprehensible to me. I didn't doubt the oysters would go down but it hardly seemed comfortable.

'I expect it was so they could sprint for a feather. You know, the vomitorium,' Chrissy said.

'Easier to get up off your side,' she went on, when I looked puzzled. 'A kind of rolling start. Like a western roll.' That was the latest kind of high jump and only one of the class, Faith, had mastered it. We were not very athletic either. Still we had produced Gilberte.

'How do you know, silly?'

'I tried it one night when I was necking. At least I imagined it. I imagined I was Arria reclining with Paetus.'

'I can't imagine you and spotty Jeff committing suicide one after the other.'

'At least acne is a sign of puberty.'

'Post-puberty I should have thought you meant. Unless Jeff is rather backward . . .'

'No, he's not backward. I should think Jeff could teach the Romans a thing or two.'

Chrissy had got up and flounced off.

Gilberte was lying on her stomach with *The Mathematical Theory of Relativity* in front of her. She gave no indication of listening. She had the concentration of a blinkered horse, or the serenity, once she had pushed off, of the Lady of Shalott.

'*On either side the river lie, Long fields of barley and of rye, That clothe the wold and meet the sky,*' I said under my breath and she looked up. 'I'm sorry, I didn't mean to interrupt.'

'It's all right,' she said. 'I'm just killing time before I have to go and see the headmistress.'

'I always think those are the best lines, don't you? The beginning. Even better than the mirror, the scenery she floats through.'

'Except at that stage she hasn't seen it, it's like a tapestry.'

'I hadn't thought of that. Do you mind if I use it in an essay?'

'Go ahead. I'm not doing it anyway.'

I looked at her admiringly, because she gave me a chase in English too.

'This interview with the headmistress. If you want to talk about it . . .'

'No. It's too complicated. It's a family matter really. But thanks.'

'Are you going to the school dance?'

'I expect so.'

I was trying to get my mother to let me wear one of my dancing costumes, an Hungarian skirt with a dark navy border. She was doubtful but it seemed to me ideal for a barn dance. At any moment I might resort to the first movement of an Hungarian czardas: a hauteur so amazing a passing peasant would be frozen in his tracks or wish to be eaten by a bear.

What happened with the headmistress I never heard, because we were preoccupied with the barn dance, but I gathered it was one of several interviews. The headmistress was working on Gilberte's father to let her go to university; this was common knowledge but not why Gilberte should be cloistered in the office with its imposing traffic symbols: STOP, WAIT, COME IN. I'm not even sure now if those were the messages: Stop may have meant It's Useless Today and Wait may have implied the headmistress would be available in ten minutes. It was a modern invention and it went with the new school assembly hall we had clambered over with the headmistress. Hadn't she said on the one occasion she taught us, that we were the crème de la crème because we took Latin.

The week before the barn dance I had worked with Faith on a spider's web of string to hang over the bar. I was so preoccupied with boys, whether one would approach me in my Hungarian skirt, that the cobweb was soon over-ornate and well on the way to being lace. It brought gusts of laughter from the others but I couldn't stop myself weaving.

The attitude of Gilberte's father seemed to be that boys went to university if they were so inclined and girls were homemakers and married. The fact that one of his sons had had a motorbike accident that week and the other had left school without any qualifications made no difference. If they had wished to go . . . The headmistress, whose own father had been doting, was at a loss. A meeting, an impromptu visit, perhaps at some hour designed to show her superiority - this would be a little unfair on Gilberte's mother who might be caught peeling potatoes.

'Is there a family history of illness, any debility?' the headmistress had asked as she chain-smoked. 'Anything that might make an academic career a necessary protection?'

But Gilberte couldn't think of anything. She sat, not unlike her mother, with her hands in her lap and her fair head downcast; she was not even thinking of the dance since she was, besides the brightest girl in class, also the tallest. Statistics were against there being many tall boys.

'You *would* like to go, Gilberte?' the headmistress asked. 'To spend the next three years studying maths or science?'

'Pure mathematics. I should like to study pure mathematics.'

'I took Greats,' the headmistress said, fitting a fresh cigarette into her ebony holder. Girls had been expelled from the bushes for less.

'Punting - of course there are no punts in Auckland, or wherever it is you would be going. We must find the best professor. Perhaps I could write to him. It is the final school that produces the best days of your life.'

When Gilberte still said nothing and continued to look at her hands the headmistress said 'I'll write to your father and ask him to call one evening.'

Adamantine, the headmistress thought. That is what Gilberte's father is. But how to deal with him? His love of figures; the genetic brilliance that had skipped his sons and alighted on the head of his daughter; the scandal of a talent gone to waste. She foresaw it would be useless to pick the wrong option; it was like a lucky dip. She must have a word to the science mistress about genetics. There was a rumour that one of the sons was up before the magistrate.

I managed to get my Hungarian skirt out of my mother and there were enough short boys for partners so I disowned the cobweb. A large black spider was fastened in the centre of it. There was one very tall boy for Gilberte and between dances we sat out on haybales beneath the parallel bars. There was a line between her brows and she seemed, who was adept at every combination of atoms, to be concentrating on the M.C.

The next day Gilberte was called out of the double period of science and when she returned her eyes were red. The barn dance had given me an insight into valencies: the inept and hesitant way male and female hands joined - some of the boys should wear gloves, Chrissy had complained, and others held your hand like a wet fish - made me think that elements too knew an initial hesitancy which was only overcome at the last moment, possibly by an external director. But the boldest atoms seized their partners round the waist and swept them into an embrace.

We were sitting under the library trees again, discussing boys. There was Beatrice knitting a complex sweater for her boyfriend - they were so committed they seemed almost married: her tall hairy-legged boyfriend need only don long trousers, sweater and a pipe and I saw them settled for life. At the end-of-year senior ball the headmistress and senior mistresses sat on the stage in rows, wearing their academic gowns. 'A last warning what we have missed,' Chrissy would say.

Whether the headmistress wore her gown at her interviews with Gilberte's father, I am not sure. There were several interviews.

Sometimes Gilberte's mother came too, though she probably added very little. Gilberte herself, apart from stating her love of mathematics, probably said little as well; perhaps the headmistress was hoping for an impassioned plea, a little Marie Curie. But the father remained adamant. Gilberte's gifts were of course a compliment to his own bent for figures, a gift which nature had not bestowed on his sons. But he believed it should be regarded as nothing more than a fluke. Here the headmistress must have resisted the desire to press the STOP button under her desk or to catapult him from his chair, a device that was not yet installed. 'She has the heart and soul of her mother,' she thought. The father's success was beginning to seem very conditional.

'Gilberte,' she counselled the quiet lank girl, giving up part of her lunch hour and asking that coffee be brought, an unheard-of compliment. She felt as if she might be fighting for the life of a future Nobel Prize winner. In that case a special board would have to be made to go alongside the Dux and Excellence in Work and Sport. 'You must fight, with whatever strength you've got. You are not strong and the sheltered life of the academy, the introductions to young men who would understand your merit, the attentions of professors, after the first anonymous year in a class of five hundred pure mathematicians, would give you the security I fear you need. Your father's idea of security is quite a different thing.'

'Do you see me married to an academic?' Gilberte asked, casting an eye towards Beatrice's knitting and drawing her long legs further under her so she was inside the valency of shade cast by the tree.

'The headmistress seems to think I should. Be grateful, I mean.'

'You haven't had much to compare one with. Have you ever met a professor?'

'I suppose Dr Petrovsky could be an example.'

'I certainly don't fancy Dr Petrovsky. We're all terrified of him.'

'Of course he is no longer engaged in research which may be the cause of his bad temper. And the fact that we don't do our homework. You do, of course.'

'I think she means someone quiet and dreamy who will smile when I mention the pleasure of numbers. Someone in the same field to talk projective geometry with in the evenings. Do you think that is likely?'

'I think she wants to see you protected. Like a rare white albino. Or the class unicorn. Then when you are justly famous she can put your name on a board outside her office, like a stuffed moose.'

She smiled suddenly and I couldn't tell whether it was maths she was thinking of, or the moose.

The end of the year was nearly on us. Our final exams were over and a few lazy weeks were left. One by one we had trooped to visit the careers advisor and those who were not obviously nurses or teachers, a minority, were advised to supplement their skills with typing classes. I sat in the back of a fourth-form class and mastered the keyboard in the last term. Chrissy was going to be a dental technician; Beatrice put down her knitting long enough to enroll for physiotherapy. 'I suppose you'll treat your patients like wool strung on needles,' Chrissy had called out and for a moment I had a vision of a Heath Robinson contraption and legs in white plaster.

One day I walked with Gilberte around the field above the boarding school. A few sixth formers, those who had not been accredited, were walking about, talking to themselves with books tightly closed, or lying face down on the bleached grass.

'Romantic, isn't it?' I said. 'Though not to the swots.'

'I suppose they've come up here to escape distractions. Those who have passed can be rather cruel.'

'A life passed in study and learned pursuits. Rather nun-like in a way. I suppose they are not allowed to go to dances either.'

'At least if they pass they will have done it on their own merits. Or so the headmistress says.'

I remembered a time I had heard her console a weeping girl who had failed some exam with a terse: 'It's only a year in your life, child. What a fuss over a year!'

One lunch hour I escaped before the bell and walked to a French pastry shop at the corner and filled my capacious black umbrella with meat pies which we ate under the trees. Why in the years at school had I not been more daring, I wondered. I was going to be a librarian and take some extra-mural units. In a few weeks I would be overdressed and sitting surrounded by pots of paste, invisible tape and date slips, with a pile of dog-eared books beside me as I learned 'to mend'.

I would be at the prize-giving but not the last assembly. One more singing of brutal *Gaudeamus*, so much less charitable than Shakespeare's seven stages of man, though Shakespeare tended to overdo senility. A speech about achievement and the headmistress in a stunning sheath over which her cap and gown presided like a presentiment of the mighty wing. She was rumoured to be highly nervous because of the presence of the Board of Governors.

But Gilberte was not at the prize-giving. Not there to receive her dux's ring and to go up last on the stage where the lower ranks had gone in threes and twos. There was a rumour that her father had taken her away from school and she was going to be his secretary. The headmistress made a little speech of regret which I thought was tinged with anger and her speech was on the wastage of women's abilities, a wastage she had given her life to prevent, though at the same time she set a reassuring example of smoking and drinking gin and tonic. I think that was why we respected her. I've never forgotten the day it was my turn in her office and I found her sitting in her exclusive underwear behind the desk, lighting one cigarette from the stub of another. 'Don't stare, girl,' she said. 'Can't you see I've spilt my coffee. We can carry on as though nothing has happened.'

'What is *your* side of the story?' she used to say to a girl sent out to stand in a corridor and eventually led to her office, like a fly to a spider. But Gilberte had gone and Gilberte's father had lain still and escaped by his superior masculine strength. Her speech had an edge that evening, a pace like Keats composing in top form.

Beatrice told me what had happened. She was a boarder and she had witnessed more of the evening meetings than the rest of us who were day-girls. It seemed the headmistress, though it was a little hard to tell from a distance, had extended her hand in what seemed a gesture of goodwill and further meetings and then at the last moment her hand had struck Gilberte's father's face.

'It sounds like science fiction,' I said disbelievingly, when we were sitting in a coffee bar during my lunch hour. 'Are you sure you were not mistaken?'

But she swore it was true. 'It was like that Ngaio Marsh story where the sky turns black when you've killed a rabbit.'

But I preferred to think that the headmistress had been seized by Gilberte's love of mathematics and her hand had risen in the shape of the first numeral.

All I know of Gilberte is what Chrissy told me. She married the first man she met at a dance, had five children, and ran a fish and chip shop. At least she could add the numbers in her head.

JUDY McNEIL

No . . . Not Marilyn Monroe!

Marilyn had spent a whole year of her life photographing her children and things that were broken. She'd had the children standing on chairs, leaning against trees, laughing, fighting, posing. She'd photographed their hands and feet, their headless bodies, even their reflections in mirrors. Then she'd taken the broken leadlight door that she'd put her shoulder through, and photographed it from every possible angle. She'd arranged broken cups, singly, in rows, in piles and captured burnt pots and handleless jugs on her film.

After all this was done she'd fixed them in a photograph album to look at, reflect upon, wondering why? Why this life and not that? She'd even captured her own misshapen body – too large around the middle – breasts sagging into stomach, jaw melding into neck and began to find it beautiful.

Cups were important objects. Her favourites were always either blue or yellow. Blue for when she was feeling strong and quiet, yellow for her gay, flamboyant self. She had one matching pair, yellow with green spots and green with yellow spots. She hated the way her friends would always choose the yellow one – leaving her the green, making her feel earthy, stolid, working-class, like an A.R.A. uniform, when she knew she was exciting.

Once, she was most pissed off with a flatmate who stoned, had broken her favourite blue cup, a gift from her sister, special. No class, this person who could adopt then break her best cup. A disturbing influence, unsettling her cool existence, taking over more than a flatmate should.

Once in a time of harmony, she'd bought three pink cups to share with two women flatmates. These cups had lasted longest, still one remaining with a few chips.

This preoccupation with broken things worried her. There was always part of her that wanted it to be nice. No chips, cracks or breaks. At one of those times she'd bought a white tea-set and locked it away for special occasions. Recently, after its use at a family afternoon tea, her present flatmate had asked where she had acquired the hospital cups. Hurt, she'd locked them away again. After her marriage had broken up she'd systematically smashed the dinner-set and the best china. She'd called it therapy. It helped her deal with the divorce procedures.

Now she was looking at broken remains on film, captured for a lifetime. Her mother had a china cabinet. Last time she'd been home her stepfather had carefully pointed out how one small section of one shelf alone was worth five thousand dollars. She wondered how he'd value her photographs. How also would he value the parts of her children? How much was a human head, hand or arm worth?

She did not have to wonder at her obsession with photographing her children. She loved every inch of their bodies. The gentle fall of a plump arm, the stoop of concentrating shoulders, a rabbit-toothed grin – all were so familiar yet so soon forgotten with passing years. Their value was obvious. They were so smooth, so round, so whole. She knew she'd never have to fix them. Not one tiny part. One thing she'd done well was forming these human creatures.

But the broken things, they needed care and attention, too. She knew she'd let it go too far for too long. Soon she would have to begin some mending.

CYNTHIA THOMAS

Another Colour

It was in Dubrovnik. I was in the square buying some fruit for lunch. The day was very hot and I was sticky and not in a very good mood. The oranges to the side of the stall were sliced in half, I supposed to attract the wasps. They were everywhere. So were the people. I felt very foreign, though in reality I suppose that over half of them must have been tourists, like myself. But they didn't look out of place. One somehow imagines that Yugoslavians, with their strange and various history, would look different, but they didn't at all, not that I could see. These were urban people, and urban people all look alike. The sweat and heat were in my eyes. As I turned, the city walls circled me, and I saw you, silhouetted against the blue, up a long flight of stairs through a narrow alley. You were standing still, and caught in a collage of colour and ancient stone, newly whitened. At such a distance, you were beautiful.

It was in Dubrovnik that we climbed down the rock face and swam under the gaze of the city walls. We exclaimed at the sea rectangled before us. It was more than blue. It was another colour. It was bottomless, and salty, and we floated easily on our backs, saying nothing. Occasionally I opened my eyes and dared to look into the white sun. Vertical again, I could see that you had floated a long way away. There was a brilliant white, terraced hotel across the bay. It had its own private pool, a piece of sea fenced off. You wanted to piss into the sea because you knew it would reach the rich people through the wire, sooner or later.

Remember that we gained an hour in Yugoslavia. We came to Skopje on the train from Thessaloniki, and stayed at the Studentski Dom for two days. When the time came to catch the bus to Dubrovnik, we were an hour early. Time didn't seem to matter much then, although it probably did. So we possessed a whole hour we never knew we had, and we spent it playing poker. I lost, but you always were a cheat.

It was in Dubrovnik that we recalled our own land, and wished then that we might walk through its peace for a time. Tired and dirty, crouched outside the supermarket, leaning back against the glass of the bookstore, you saw the reflection of a *Time* magazine, in English. There had been a snap election, and our party had won, several weeks past. The left seemed on the rise again. We danced and laughed with it, until the scorching heat of the early afternoon reminded us how cool it would be in the bush, and that we were a billion miles from home.

My father is a bastard. Everyone knows it, yet he is still reasonably well liked by acquaintances, and loved by his strange little family, largely because of his sense of humour. He often talks about how he started with nothing, grew up tough, knew the ways of the world, not as an example of the dream – work hard and you'll succeed – because he still has nothing, and calls everyone else bastards because of it. How big a bastard a person actually is depends largely on the make and price of their car, so it is possible to rise in the bastard stakes by going from a Mini to a Jag. All tories are necessarily bastards. So are hippies. Maoris are definitely bastards. A Maori doctor is a bastard with a degree. Anyone who looks different is one. Children can be them if they ride their bicycles over our soggy front lawn. Next door neighbours are always bastards, and so are people who attend church. Mechanics are inevitably them, and the biggest ones of all are those who are both from the largest city, and in the highest tax bracket – I mean, you'd have to be a bastard to want to live there! The only way that it is possible to surpass this highest accolade of bastardry is to phone up at dinner time.

'Who's the fucking bastard ringing at this time of night? Can't a man get any bloody peace in this world?'

'Don't worry, Dad, it'll be for me.'

'Well, tell him he's a prick.'

'Okay.'

'I haven't got many spuds.' This is directed at my mother, who has cooked almost every evening for thirty-odd years. The criterion for a good meal is first, how much of the plate it covers, but it also must be carbohydrate-laden, and include thick, red meat.

'Here, have one of mine.' She picks a potato off her plate and puts it on his. She is not really annoyed yet; this is normal. She has always taken the burnt chop. I was growing up, and had my own problems. I realized that she was a woman only when she started buying herself a few things, personal things, after we had started leaving home, giving her resources, time, and perhaps a little more peace.

'I don't want your bloody potato, woman.' He puts it back.

'I don't want it either.' The potato is getting cold and soggy.

'Oh, shit on it all.' He takes the loaf of bread and throws it at the wall. We, his children, start to laugh and kick each other under the table. Mum starts to laugh. Finally, after first feeling resentful, he joins in naturally. We eat our dinner. Later, my mother will clean the kitchen, prepare lunches, fold laundry and make shopping lists. We, the rest, sit in the lounge, watch television, do homework and squabble over whose turn it is to dry the dishes. My mother always washed. Sometimes I think that that was the only peace she ever got, alone in the evenings in the darkened kitchen.

When you came to the door that day my father went to his bedroom and shut the door. He thought, you see, that I was doing it on purpose, to irk the parent, to abort the plan for neat, white grandchildren. To be perfectly honest, I still don't feel that I consciously made a decision in favour of you at all. When I looked up, you were just, well, there – in all your smooth chocolate-ness, and you were smiling at me and all of a sudden we were together. And when we went to Europe my father was ill, and refused even to say goodbye. I thought, if my Dad dies while I'm away I'll be damned for all time. But my father didn't die. Just other things.

You said that Dubrovnik was a beautiful fairytale town, and that we would have a nice time there. I didn't want to believe you, having been disillusioned before, but when the grind of that mountain was beaten and it lay before me, down many miles, I crouched at the window and my puzzle-book fell to the floor. A little thing against the blue, nestled in a huge vastness. You said that that didn't make sense, but it did. The Pearl of the Adriatic, and the sweat hung from us. You said that the dog chiselled in the cloistered stonework looked as though it was biting its bum, and the guide looked suitably shocked. But the water drew us again, along Marsala Tito and to the rocks below; floating under an impeccable ceiling of bright light.

The *Time* magazine had in it an article about a man in America who went to McDonalds and shot all the people there. He was annoyed because he had just lost his job. I stared and stared at the pictures of blood and bodies, and the man himself, an ordinary chap, to see if I could recognize anything of myself there. You said that the sun was getting to me, and that the next day we would head for Sarajevo. I didn't know it then, but it too would be another colour, and it would be raining.

It was cool there, but it was raining. We had passed through several mountain villages on the way, and you laughed at me when I said I thought the people looked deformed. But they did. Many had rotting teeth, and foreheads on an ancient slope back to their hairline. They were peasant people, and several were lined and roughened and very ugly. You said that that was not the view that I should take, but it was my truth. The people scared me, because they were large and did not know my tongue and resented my foreign-ness.

We went to the Turkish quarter and were surrounded by souvenir vendors pressing in with their stock of dilapidated bargains. We chose instead to spend our money on herbal tea and burek, and when you later developed diarrhoea you didn't know which to blame. Even after the funicular, which I thought would hurl us off into a disagreeable and unknown space, the city from Mt Trebevic was still shrouded in mist, and I despaired at not being able to get a good photograph. On the way down in the cable car, there was a box, and on the box a notice which read, 'If car stops, open box for further instructions.' I felt my suspended fragility, and wanted to open the box, but you said there might be an alarm which would tell on us. There was no snow on the Olympic bob-sled run. It was summer, after all.

And then, suddenly one day, out of the blue, you said it was all my fault. You said that when you were at school, all your teachers wanted you to go to training college. You were the only Maori in the sixth form, and you said you failed on purpose, and went to work at the glassworks instead. You said that you wanted to be different, but ended up the same. You said that all along you had been surrounded by people like me and, now that you were here, you were surrounded by Yugoslavians; always surrounded by people who were not you. I never realized you felt your race quite so much. You frightened me. You were frightened. You said that wherever you went in the world, you would always be a minority, so instead you were going home to be alone. I thought that perhaps you were joking, but in the morning all I had was your crumpled, misspelt note in all its nothingness, and my pack and myself again. I looked down at my skin and I was very, very white. I shone out at myself. In that second I believe I was very nearly blinded. But when, later that day, I stepped outside and along and into the Turkish quarter again, yes, I could still feel my white-ness seething, but it wasn't like you said at all. The different people and the people who were different surrounded me, and I felt alone and quite scared. But not defeated – don't think that, Billy. I felt unique and strong and I was myself again after all that time under you, and my white-ness faded a bit and I was myself again. In a way, I suppose, you were right – your colour isn't mine, and what's mine isn't yours, but Christ, Billy, whatever that had to do with it I'll never know.

It was in Dubrovnik that I loved you most of all, I think. Now I am alone. It doesn't feel like you said it would. Now that I am alone, now that you have told me that I am to be of no further use to you, and I am alone and have acknowledged the fact, I will take a deep breath. And with that, I will know that I am still alive, and I will not stop living because some boy I once knew refuses now to be intimate. Already I can see another colour, and it is not blue, or grey, as you might have wished or supposed in thinking that I needed you only to lean on. In fact, it's not any colour that you ever told me about, Billy. It's not your colour and it's not mine and it belongs to nobody. It is a colour far, far brighter than that. It is one of the bright colours, and I can see it rising over Parahaki and spreading out to touch me. If I look hard enough I can see it in my bloodstream, surging out to my extremities. It is another colour.

JAN KEMP

Born Moments

Yes! Yes! She's first-class-honours material. Congratulations. 'A' plus. Wax-sealed and mortar-boarded. But no, she isn't. Who is that bright girl curled up on the bed at Student Health, her exam paper naked on her desk in the exam room? What is that huge red and black pill she has just swallowed with the water the nurse brought in? Librium to calm her down, Valium to make her feelings stop just above her heart so that she can't feel them. So they can't confuse her. Mogadon to make her sleep at night, to stop those notions whirling round inside her head. Mogadon to soothe her mind into a false sleep to wake dry-mouthed as late as ten o'clock to drink down the valium.

'The function of the imagination in the ability of the individual to orient herself in a constantly incipient cosmos.' Where did your essay's title come from? Oh, oh? That? From my friend Paul's mouth. Paul sat on his desk, stoned. Oh, oh, Paul, Pauline asked, what shall I call my essay. Call it this, said Paul and made the words trip off his tongue. Hard words. Meaningless words. Words with edges and no faces. No energy in them. Pauline will call her essay that. They want that, up at the word factory. Up there at the word factory, they make trapezes out of dead words. And Pauline's supposed to wear her spangled intelligence suit and swing between them with the greatest of ease. She's just a head. There she sits, a huge head at a desk. Tubes fill her with the glucose of knowledge. Her frail body is limp. No longer does she walk or run. At the word factory, you're just a head.

Why didn't they tell Pauline life was going to be like this? Who gives out the instructions? Searching, searching through all those books for someone to say something that she understands. Where can she connect? Where do they write about young women in love and say what to do? Which health nurse explains about contraception best? If she has a lover, she might get pregnant if she doesn't take the pill. If she takes the pill she is not herself, feels all choked up. Men don't like wearing condoms. They feel all choked up. You can't use other forms of contraception until you've had a baby. Pauline hasn't had one. Do you want a lover? Do you want sex? What's free love? What's this dark velvet flower between her legs? Whose are those arms around her? Whose cock is pushing, pushing into her velvet flower, caressing her, so that she's full up and not empty any more?

Did you know, lover, that yesterday she couldn't believe the sun would rise? Yesterday, she'd read and read all those notions thinking people had about life, that there's no hope. How could Pauline hope any longer, her head full of other people's hopelessnesses? Where did her own hope go? Where are her own thoughts?

Pauline was a happy little girl and played tennis. Until that day at the lake in the photograph. You remember the one. The other people's daughter had a corduroy dress and a handbag. She was slim. She could see over her tummy and watch her toes curl. Pauline couldn't. Her tummy always got in the way. Pauline had a tweed skirt. Why wasn't she too slim in a corduroy dress with a handbag? Oh, oh. Let Pauline fall in the lake and drown. Her big tummy will make her float. It will be her water-wings and make her stay floating. She'll float forever and never be able to drown.

Pauline is a foundling. Why otherwise is she ugly? Why otherwise does her mind slip off? Why otherwise when she meets nice boys does she either say nothing or spill over so that they are washed away? Remember Jim Hopa, the Maori boy with the handsome face? Judy arranged it. Pauline was to sit next to him on the bench at playtime. There he was, waiting. Pauline, her heart in her throat, sat down. Pauline spilled over. She asked him things. He didn't answer. Just grunted. She should have said nothing. The other girls don't talk when they sit on the bench next to their boyfriends. They smile and now and then smirk a bit and then the boyfriend tells a joke. Then the girl laughs and her eyes sparkle and she looks away. But she never says anything, Blabbermouth.

Aegrotat. That's all you're worth. Aegrotat. They passed you. An honours degree with an aegrotat. You'd been there so long they had to pass you. How can you hold up your face? You who ran out of the tutorial and wanked in the toilet? Paul said the best thing to do when you feel like coming is to wank. Go for the feeling, Paul said. Let it out! If your lover's not around, wank! It's all pleasure! That's all it is. Paul is a hedonist. Paul can eat drugs as if they were licorice allsorts. Pauline can't. Her threshold is too insecure. Paul sits on the window sill. He takes a trip. On her best days Pauline can talk to Paul as he sits on the window sill, dangling his legs outside over the ginger plant at midnight. They have their best talks then. Intricate talks about reality. Together they float through the eye of a needle.

Pauline is sitting on the couch looking at the lily Paul stuck in the fire grate. She has just broken up with her lover. She is a flower on the couch faded into the furnishings. Paul bosses her round. 'I'm taking you for a ride on my scooter, Pauline; come on, no is no answer.' Pauline clutches Paul's body. The wind goes through her hair. The Domain trees unfurl a green corridor. They go to the scented gardens for the blind. They are blind people too, sniffing. Such sweetness. Such honey. Paul showed her how to live. Sniff the scented flowers.

When they first moved into the flat, there was Pauline's bed, her old stereo, a few records and Paul's picture of Venus on her shell from an art book. He'd stuck it into an old wooden frame from a junk-shop and cellotaped the back down. They hung it up. They put Corelli on the stereo and lay down on the bed. Paul smoked a joint. His hair was soft on the pillow beside Pauline's. He smelt like lavender. He was Pauline's best friend. The girls in the picture danced. One of them held a laurel twig between her teeth. Corelli's sounds drew invisible shapes that were the choreography of the dance in the air above the bed. Synaesthesia. The beautiful graces danced for them as Paul and Pauline lay there watching. Paul said, 'What mind can make such an image of beauty?' Paul always knew what to say. He said things and Pauline would breathe agreement. And then, she might have an idea too.

Paul and Pauline rode up Mount Eden. To the top. Paul took a trip. They saw the sun through mist. It was white as the moon above the crater. They sat on the green-grassed crater's edge and looked at it. It was a white hole. 'Paul, there's the way out!' They might have flown like Chagall lovers in trees over the crater and out through the hole in the sky. It is only a canopy, the sky. They wouldn't have to knock against it any more or be bruised by bumping against the earth. The membrane of the white sky had made a tunnel. They could leave. 'Oh Paul, let's go!' But he was feeling too fragile for flying. Pauline drove the wobbling scooter home, Paul on the pillion, clutching her. Then Paul sat in the walnut chair they'd stripped to the natural wood. Pauline sat on his bed. 'Look at me Pauline, you must not take your eyes off me for a split second. Every second is so painful to me if you look away, for I am only a moment old. Oh Pauline, look at me.'

So all night for hours, Pauline looked into Paul's amber eyes, trying not to blink. She could sense the gulf he slid down into when she had to blink. She tried to keep him talking. He was made of a thin, thin thread, like the first strand of a cobweb. He could only think single lines. 'Dear Paul,' Pauline kept saying, 'I am here with you.'

'I am made of light,' Paul said. 'I am the first breath of the universe. Don't fall asleep Pauline, I will be so lonely if you fall asleep.'

Pauline propped herself up on the strawberry cushion.

'You are red and green,' Paul said. 'Your face is flaming with red flames and green flames. 'You are so beautiful,' he said. 'Have you just been born a moment, like me?'

'Yes,' Pauline said.

'Don't look away from my eyes! Oh Pauline, don't look away. If you knew of the pain, you'd never look away.'

Pauline looked into his strange amber eyes full of pain, determined to look forever if she had to. What would become of them? Two new breaths looking forever into each other's eyes. They could blow away.

'The sun will rise soon,' Pauline said. 'Let's go and watch it, Paul.'

'Yes, do let's,' said Paul. He took her hand. They walked awkwardly outside, still staring into each other's eyes in case it hurt him. They fumbled their way down the dim passage through the porch and out on to the lawn under the apple tree, where they could sit and watch the sun rise over the corrugated roofs of houses that were tucked in, like theirs, against the hill. They sat on the grass like Hansel and Gretel. The sun came up. Paul was enchanted with the colours.

Then Pauline led him gently back inside and put him to bed. She peered into his amber eyes that were more like cat's diamonds than ever and stroked his soft hair. He blinked once or twice. He closed his eyelids.

'It's all right now, Pauline,' he said. 'The pain is gone. I can close my eyes and watch the kaleidoscope inside my head. You sleep now, you've had enough.'

The next night they went to a party. They rode on the scooter to the house where Pauline played the piano between lectures in the daytime when no one was home. Allison said, 'You two are of one mind.' Allison was wearing her silk dress from the junk-shop. 'You two are of one mind,' she kept saying to them, all evening.

'Then so we are!' Paul laughed. He didn't believe in anything except what happens in the present. For there isn't anything else. 'Now is there?' Paul would ask, his hands turned out, asking too.

Pauline loved Paul and Paul loved Pauline. But they couldn't be lovers. It just didn't work. Paul really preferred boys. Or maybe boys and perhaps a girl. They'd been at his parents' place in Eketahuna. His mother had made dainty scones for their morning tea. Pauline had slept in the spare room. They thought she was a nice companion for Paul. They were European immigrants and had an accent.

Paul and Pauline would go to the river and he'd get stoned. Then, they'd play. He put on a beret. She gave him a name. 'You are Pierre Hugonet à la cloche,' she said, though it made no sense.

'And you,' he said twirling invisible moustaches, 'are Nymphet Paradoxine!' They giggled and invented stories all afternoon with their new names on like badges.

They hitch-hiked back to Auckland. They stopped in New Plymouth and stayed the night in Paul's friend's friend's place. Actors. All gay. All gentle. They had to sleep in Hewie's bed. Hewie was away in Wellington, rehearsing, away from the big panelled house with soft lights. It was a single bed with a scooped shape. They met in the scoop. Paul had put Beethoven's Ninth on the stereo. They smoked a joint in the bed. They tried to make love, but Pauline kept imagining Paul was a platypus and giggled. Paul kept slipping off just as they'd got started. They both laughed.

'It doesn't matter,' he said.

They lay giggling in the bed, while Beethoven's Ninth loomed in grand gestures through the air and through the mattress and through their bodies. The music went slower and slower. Between each chord there was a huge space where a crater or avalanche might have fallen.

'Oh, oh!' Paul called out in mock pain. 'This is *too* much, Pauline!' He laughed and leapt out of bed, pulling his red singlet over his bottom and between his legs like a jump-suit and held it there. 'Am I respectable?' Then laughed and let go of the singlet and took a Nureyev leap to the stereo.

'Hey, hey, Nymphet!' he yelled. 'Beethoven's been playing on 78!'

LUCINDA BIRCH

Birds

1

I begin with the end: It was mid-winter and still dusty on the gravel road. The fat red-headed driver had left the door of the bus open so that you could hear the wheels go round, shh shh shh, and watch the painted tops of the rickety batten fence flash by like a flickering line of white cabbage butterflies. Gorse and manuka grew from the steep mountain-sides that pushed up on either side of the road; a few pink and yellow flowers fighting for a spot in the sun, yellow winning. I was going home, my farewells over and my friend flown away, like a bird. Ahead of the bus a hawk sliced through the air like a slow-motion circular saw. Lower and lower until it was barely above the ground, its claws trailed over the stones, then grabbed and pulled at the stringy flesh of the carcass lying there, entrails spread through the dust and flattened by passing cars.

2

It is a few days earlier: My friend is packing and her mother brings me a cup of tea as I sit outside watching the lake in front of their house. It is too hot to drink tea, sweat breaks out under the hair that lies damply across my forehead. The winter sun seems closer and brighter than usual, my eyes hurt. On the still and dirty lake water-birds float and flap, unable to fly because their wings have been cut off, clipped. Two white swans circle each other, their necks snaking back and forth, their shortened wings open wide. I sip my tea and watch as they swim round and round, heads dipping and bowing, water spraying. Until finally one climbs on to the other and they fuck clumsily. (It is hard to balance with short wings.) It doesn't take long. When they are finished they circle each other again, intertwining gently and touching red beaks together to form a heart shape with their long pale necks.

3

Later, at the airport: My friend and I say our final goodbye. We are sitting with plastic cups full of weak coffee in plastic chairs by a window. Outside is a small garden of marigolds, and a lawn of dry and dying grass. We talk of trivial things. I stare out the window and wonder why people always have to leave. When did life stop being all hellos and start being all goodbyes. I am feeling sorry for myself. A little yellow bird is pecking at the ground close to the orange border of marigolds. Before I have time to warn it, wave or yell, a magpie swoops from nowhere and pins the smaller bird to the ground on its back. It screeches and struggles as the magpie, using its beak like a dagger, stabs again and again and again. I jump up, knocking my chair over and waving my arms shouting shoo shoo. The magpie doesn't take any notice. The little yellow bird has stopped moving and the magpie is pulling tufts of skin and feathers from its stomach. I clap hopelessly and the magpie looks at me sideways, grabs the yellow bird in its dagger-beak and hops arrogantly out of sight.

LUCINDA BIRCH

After

She lay in bed beside him naked under a sheet one blanket and a bedcover. She lay on her side. Facing away from him. One of her legs lay on top of the other, knees pressing together, jigsaw pieces that didn't fit, painful. Her arms folded up hands tucked under her chin. Her stomach and breasts tumbled in soft layers rolling hills on to the sheet below. If she died a purple-black bruise would grow there, on the downhill side of her body. She tried not to move. She breathed in shallow sips so that her lungs wouldn't rock her chest. She pleaded silently with her heart to quieten its thudding. Her skin prickled but she didn't dare scratch. The wetness flowed from between her legs and made the bed cold and uncomfortable but she didn't dare move. She lay still, very still.

The man beside her twitched, took one or two snuffling breaths and went to sleep.

She sat watching two prostitutes talking and laughing in the shopping mall. They looked like birds of paradise. Other people in the mall turned to look as they were passing. The two women preened under the attention. She envied their guts. She envied their bodies, tightly encased in shining colours. She envied their hair, gaudily dyed orange and glossy blue-black. She envied their faces the lipstick the colour of scarlet geraniums. She envied their confidence their cynicism their bitterness. She envied the money they earned.

The man beside her twitched, took one or two snuffling breaths, rolled over and went back to sleep.

She lay in bed beside him naked under a sheet one blanket and a bedcover. She lay on her side. Facing away from him. She lay still, very still.

The Unusual Meanderings
by Merry Bone
of Flavia River....

Silvery

♡

Dear Reader,

(O Godde will they like me i am only little 6.
stupid inside & i have to get the baby
her toast.)

The dog is in here doing smelly farts he
is tied up to the chromium plated
cupboard support system he
BITES POSTGIRLS

the baby is pulling at my skirt i am   eating
a bit of marmite →
here is the marmite

Photo by Judy Jan
Rogers Jan '88

Fairy
Rabbit
my
11
year
old →
magic
now
I told her it was life

has just →
touch
then
& death

ME ?

ANGELA WHEN DAWN ...

started playing the piano she has the
she has been a bit woolly til
she dedicated herself completely.
in this hard hard hard hard world.
i have got a pimple on my

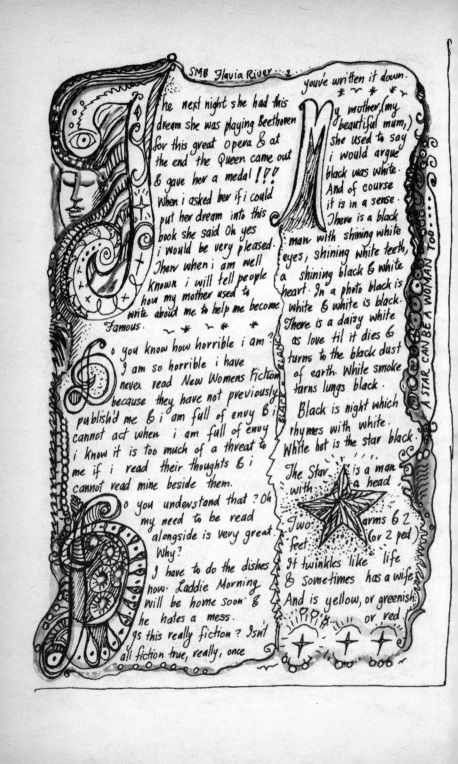

The next night she had this dream she was playing Beethoven for this great opera & at the end the Queen came out & gave her a medal !?! When i asked her if i could put her dream into this book she said Oh yes i would be very pleased. Then when i am well known i will tell people how my mother used to write about me to help me become famous.

* ~ * ~ * ~

Do you know how horrible i am? I am so horrible i have never read New Womens Fiction because they have not previously publish'd me & i am full of envy & i cannot act when i am full of envy i know it is too much of a threat to me if i read their thoughts & i cannot read mine beside them.

Do you understand that? Oh my need to be read alongside is very great. Why? I have to do the dishes now. Laddie Morning will be home soon & he hates a mess. Is this really fiction? Isn't all fiction true, really, once

you've written it down.

* ~ * ~ * ~

My mother (my beautiful mum,) she used to say i would argue black was white. And of course it is in a sense. There is a black man with shining white eyes, shining white teeth, a shining black & white heart. In a photo black is white & white is black. There is a daisy white as love til it dies & turns to the black dust of earth. White smoke turns lungs black.

Black is night which rhymes with white. White hot is the star black.

The Star is a man with a head Two arms & 2 feet (or 2 ped) It twinkles like life & sometimes has a wife And is yellow, or greenish or red.

A STAR CAN BE A WOMAN TOO

BLACK IS BLACK

the shiny to think, it always makes me think.

xxxx

i love the smell of twink. Ra.

have never perceived a blue star
And a star is away very far
It comes out at night
& is quite a nice sight
it is hope in the nightness (sans Ra)

Of course Ra is actually
a star herself, but for
some reason she goes down at
night. I remember watching the
sun go down into the glittery golden
sea at Opononi & Florrie Homes
saying to me "it's a wonder it doesn't
steam." I thought that was a beautiful
image.

Well it is 20 to 2 and i have
to go & clean up now. Laddie
hasn't come home, perhaps he knows
everythings a mess.

When i was making
love with him last
night talking of
images a deep green
forest came into my consciousness
and shimmered in suspension it

SMB Flavia River 3

was so pretty hanging
there, half focussed
like a distant photo
through the poor
filter of me,
for i am full of
poison. And now i
experienced a waterfall,
a simple silver
veil, deep into the
beyond. How it
streamed, with me,
into the forest of
antiquity...

Then it was sleep, &
then it was dreams, my
lifeline to possibility...

JANET ARTHUR

My Friends the Bikies

Trevor was the older brother of the two and from what I'd heard he was elected gang president through his ability to eat his own shit.

I had a crush on the other brother Sam because he seemed more sensible and quieter than Trevor. Their only sister Leslie and I were over at their place when her two brothers arrived home with John who I took an instant dislike to. He had dark wavy hair, black freckles that stood out on his pasty face and cruel eyes. Because John fancied me I kept out of his reach.

I went to the bikies' party with Leslie's friend Mary because I thought I would be safe with Trevor and Sam there. After we had arrived at the house we all sat round drinking beer until one of the bikies decided it was time for action. The bikies all but one stripped from the waist down and Mary proceeded to perform oral sex on one while another had sexual intercourse with her at the same time. When they had gratified their lust they decided to stick a beer bottle up Mary's vagina to see how far it would go. 'That's no good,' one of them yelled, 'we can't see the blood drip down.' 'Let's stick a lemonade bottle up, aye?' another said.

For a long time before this I had been too scared to move but now my loathing was stronger. I crept away to the toilet hoping no one would notice. But John was waiting for me as I came out. 'Now it's your turn.' Terrified, I ran around the dingy room with John, still naked from the waist down, chasing me. I screamed, 'Please leave me alone. Don't!' The other bikie named Brett, who hadn't been actively involved, yelled 'Come on John, leave her.' Brett took me back to the toilet where he offered to protect me – for a price . . . The hot sickly sperm shot down my throat. He gripped my head between his hands, forcing me to choke while swallowing. I broke away just in time to vomit in the toilet. He then abused my body further by forcing me to have sex with him.

'The bastard,' I thought. 'How dare he.'

Brett and another bikie dropped us down the road from where we lived. Just before the bikies roared away on their machines, Mary kissed Brett several times. Still disgusted I thought, 'Mary might enjoy being used and dominated by these so-called men, but I would never freely submit.'

Two months later I still had a crush on Sam. I wasn't thinking about anything in particular, while slowly wandering down to the bus-stop after working overtime at the factory, when two bikes stopped right beside me. Sam asked, 'Do you want to come to a party?'

'Maybe he's noticed me after all. This is a dream come true,' I thought.

'Yes, okay. I'll come.' Sam took me to a flat Trevor and a few other bikies had moved into not long before. When I arrived I immediately noticed that John was there but because this time I could see Sam and Trevor, I knew I'd be fine. Sam suddenly disappeared into one of the bedrooms with a loud-mouthed broad who had plenty of make-up on and big boobs. My dream was short-lived. John grabbed me and forced me in to one of the unoccupied bedrooms. 'I'm going to f..k you,' he said.

'Oh god, not again.' He pushed me on the bed, I struggled and fought . . . I finally broke free and ran out into the hallway where he held me against the wall just outside the bathroom. I pleaded with him to let me go.

'I'm going to f..k the ass off you and if you don't stop trying to run away I'll bash your brains in,' he threatened.

I was aware of Trevor's voice in the bathroom. 'You'd better do what he says, he means it.' Trevor's girlfriend laughed. John led me into the vacant bedroom and laid me down . . .

When it was over I felt dirty and dead. I cried so much that the other bikie at the party must have felt sorry for me. He folded his arm around my shoulder and spoke to me softly. 'Don't worry about John. He's gone away now.' He offered me a beer and I took enough to make me forget, or so I thought. We eventually had sex at his suggestion and shortly after Sam informed me that the nice friendly bikie had venereal disease. I don't know who I held the most contempt for: Sam who invited me and must have known what lay in wait for me; his older brother whom I had grown up with and who betrayed me by suggesting I submit and who didn't lift a finger to help; Trevor's girlfriend who ridiculed a member of her own sex and herself by laughing at a situation she could one day find herself in; John who raped me, making sure he did so before the friendly bikie could have his way with me and give John V.D.; the soft-spoken bikie who offered me sympathy in a cold, calculating way so I would be the only one to catch V.D.; or finally myself, who trusted my life-long friends, who gave in to that prick John without fighting to the death, and who allowed myself to trust another so-called man only to be given a dose of V.D. I couldn't go to the police about the rape and when I told my friend Leslie she demoralized me further by saying that if it really was rape I shouldn't have had sex with anyone else. She hadn't understood that after John raped me I thought I couldn't be humiliated any more . . . I was wrong.

Some months later Leslie found her brother Sam a girlfriend. She was very pretty and, most importantly, a virgin. I didn't want to go to the bikies' flat with them because of my previous experiences. Leslie convinced me to go. Her parents would only allow her to go out with me, as I was older than her.

When we arrived, the only people there were some girlfriends of Leslie and a short bikie named Sandy. Also another bikie named Rocky was in one of the bedrooms with his live-in love. I sat and listened while Leslie and her friends all joked and talked. They must have become bored because Sandy walked over to my chair and shoved it over sideways on to the floor. Everyone laughed while I picked myself and the chair up off the floor . . . The third time it happened I was in tears. Sandy spoke. 'What's the big idea of spreading f...ing lies about my friend John raping you? You f...en slut. Caught the dose after the second f..k did you? You're a f....en slut, aren't you?' The girls taunted me with 'f...en slut' over and over. Wasn't it enough that I'd gone through the ordeal once? Why this ridicule? I wasn't allowed to forget.

As I walked out on to the stairway Rocky and his girlfriend came out of their bedroom arguing. Rocky tried to pull me into the bedroom. The others must have heard Rocky's girlfriend scream, 'Go on you slut, Rocky wants to f..k you.' I grabbed the bannister and pulled as hard as I could. The others tried to push me into Rocky's arms just for a joke. They stopped shortly afterwards and I didn't stay long enough to find out why. I flew out the front door of the flat crying all the way home. 'What's wrong with me,' I thought. 'Those bikies have put me through hell and all those bastards are blaming me. As for Leslie and those other bitches . . . they can't see that they're just like me, being used. The only difference is they enjoy it.'

Leslie and I didn't speak for a long time. Afterwards I decided that I still wanted to be her friend.

Leslie and I went to a dance in the centre of town every Saturday night and we kept away from the bikies until one night we were walking past a group of them. Leslie decided to go and have a nosey to see what they were up to. Rocky grabbed Leslie and said, 'Let's go and have a f..k.' Leslie pulled away and Rocky decided to try the same line on me. We didn't see Trevor there but he must have been concerned about Leslie's safety because he asked for two volunteers to take us home. I climbed on the back of Kevin's bike and Leslie climbed on the back of another bike. We zoomed away and one of them decided to pick something up from his place on the way. When we arrived we separated willingly. I made love to the tall blonde good-looking bikie named Kevin. I say made love because for the first time I had a sexual experience. My partner cared enough to make the experience as good for me as it was for him.

I guess I looked upon him as my knight-in-shining-armour because he took me away from what could have turned into a nasty situation, and for that I was grateful. We emerged from the bedroom to where Leslie and the other bikie were waiting. I'd never travelled fast on the back of a big bike before. What a feeling. I felt like I was flying and when Kevin dropped me off he informed me that the fastest the bike had travelled during our ride home had been one hundred and twelve miles an hour. He said he would phone me sometime soon. After I informed Leslie that I had sex with Kevin she told me that she didn't sleep with the other bikie because she didn't want to earn a bad reputation hanging around with bikies. I thought, 'What the hell are you worried about, you lost your virginity at thirteen and you've slept around with every Tom, Dick and Harry since.' Maybe it had something to do with the fact that I didn't have to take second best this time.' Kevin called me once. After that, he arranged in advance to see me on the days that suited him.

I was around at his flat when the bikies had a meeting and I stayed in his room while he went in to the lounge. When he came back I asked him what they did at this meeting. He told me that a new bikie was earning his 'Red Flags'. I was to learn much later that this meant one of the new members had to have sex with a woman who was having her period and any one of the other bikies who wanted to could have sex with her as well. While all this was going on they had an audience.

One day I was sitting talking to Kevin in his bedroom when there was a knock on the door. Kevin opened his door and this big-boobed broad that had been with Sam the night I was raped said, 'You want to come in and see this mental sheila they picked up. Rocky had just finished f...ing her when I bowled up to her and said, "What are you? A f...ing slut?" And she didn't answer so I booted her in the head. The f...ing mental bitch said she was sorry so I booted her in the head again. The f...en mental bitch.' 'What makes people like that?' I thought. 'I know who's the mental bitch.' I guess that was the first time I allowed myself to think that Kevin was just a little less than perfect.

Because I was seeing less and less of Kevin I went around to see him unexpectedly and a tall good-looking girl was standing outside his bedroom door waiting for him. I didn't let her know that I was also there to see him. A motorcycle drew up outside and the girl went down to see if it was Kevin. He had been hiding in one of the other rooms and he beckoned me in. He told me he would explain about the girl later but meanwhile I was to look out for her while he went around the road and waited.

I walked around the road with him and on the way he explained that this particular woman had held on to her virginity until she turned twenty-three and because he had taken it away from her she thought she owned him body and soul. I felt that he was hinting at me not to become too possessive. I didn't care on what terms I saw Kevin, I loved him enough to let him sleep around. I loved him too much, enough to compromise my feelings. I knew he loved me because he said 'I love you' to me. It didn't matter that there was no feeling in the way he said it. It had been the first time anyone had said those three precious words to me and I was going to fight to hang on to what they meant to me.

I became friendly with a girl named Sarah at work, who was well built and had a real nice personality. One day we sat talking and she informed me that she had met this nice quiet guy who rode a bike and she loved him so much that she was considering losing her virginity to him. After she asked me what I thought I advised her to think very carefully before surrendering and to be very sure of her feelings.

I don't know what I hoped to find when I arrived unexpectedly at Kevin's, but I knocked on his bedroom door and called his name. It took a while to sink in, but it finally dawned on me that Sarah was in there and because she described him differently from how I saw him

I hadn't realized that Kevin was the nice quiet guy she was considering losing her virginity to. I was so angry that I yelled as loud as I could, 'Get out of there fast before he f...s the ass off you.' I guess I must have stuffed up Kevin's chances because he opened up the door and booted me hard in the guts still wearing his steel-capped boots. I fell to the floor, but I quickly left the flat as a party was in full swing. I didn't want to become a victim again. Even after what Kevin had done to me I was convinced that I still loved him and the pain of not seeing him tore at my heart.

I went back only to find that Kevin had two girls living in his room because they had been thrown out of home. For some vague reason Kevin tried to convince me that he was sleeping with neither of the girls. I knew he was and I figured it must have been the girl who helped clean his bike and wore a leather jacket. If I couldn't have him, I didn't want anyone else and to prove it I took an overdose of the only medicine I had – dispirins, poisonous toothache drops, and penicillin. I was only vaguely aware of Kevin and another guy taking me to the hospital in the car. And then the pain. 'You've been a very silly girl, haven't you?' I didn't answer. 'Now this might hurt a bit,' the nurse suggested. Two people held me down while the nurse rammed a monstrous tube up my nose and down my throat. There was miles of rubber hose to swallow. I could feel the liquid gush down my stomach before I vomited it out through what room I had left in my nose and mouth. I was sure that because I hadn't succeeded in doing away with myself they were trying to do it instead by choking me. The nurse spoke again, 'Now we might not be in such a hurry to try this again.' She didn't know that my heart had been torn out, my self-respect was gone, and because I knew I wouldn't see Kevin again I just didn't care. No pain, not even extreme physical pain could compare with the pain of losing someone I never really had.

After the nurse arranged for me to see a shrink Kevin took me home in his friend's car. I guess he felt concerned because he was very careful what he said to me. I hope he had finally realized that he couldn't play with people's emotions without being responsible for the hurt they feel. He eventually married the girl who helped clean his bike.

ANNE KENNEDY

A Veil Dropped From a Great Height

Her weight is nothing to be alarmed about
An angel is her heaviest possession, apart from a piano which has hired
carrier pigeons to take its notes heavenwards.

A funeral attended by a truckload of hippies (this is 1973) was
followed in quick succession by its own death. Since then every day
in Wellington has been a public holiday – a Good Friday, a Christmas
Day, the day after.

She is leaving this city of sudden bereavements, taking her two
heaviest objects and also her two lightest; one, an ecstasy, the other,
her happiness seen from above.

A whiteness becomes black
When she was sixteen she took up sleep. She took to sleep like a duck
to water. Before that there had been no sleep to speak of. This is how
E.J. Byrne entered sleep:

Her brother, a storeman for a pharmaceutical firm, was paid in
kindness, a plastic bag full of all sorts of states. The one he offered
her was embossed on one side with a pair of closed eyelids, on the flip
side with the letter M.

'M for Mogadon, eyelids for sleep,' said E.J. Byrne. She swallowed
the white tablet with a glass of milk, its cylindrical likeness, a stack
of itself. She called through the crack in her bedroom door: 'E.J. Byrne
has taken sleep!'

E.J. Byrne sleeps. She has not slept since sleep was spoken of. Now
every night she creeps into his room. 'I must just steal forty winks.'
Every night without fail E.J. Byrne sleeps.

Everyone says sleep becomes her
In the morning there is nothing that does not match Mogadon; sheets,
shirt, knickers, socks, a dotted line on the road to school, a lined refill
that will one day make landfill. Everything is white. In the midday glare

E.J. Byrne takes three white isosceles sandwiches from a plastic bag and inspects their fillings with her protractor. They contain ninety-degree heat. 'This is the end of the white,' says E.J. Byrne, moving into the shade. Mogadon vanishes without trace – except perhaps for a half-life of speed and colour.

Now it is the afternoon and everything is very fast and colourful.

Her afternoons contain her mornings

The class is considering its centre of gravity. 'I am it!' says E.J. Byrne, putting up her hand. Her mornings, her evenings have accumulated here, about the pull of her activity. E.J. Byrne does everything there is to do at a furious pace.

In the late afternoons she plays scales prestissimo up and down the piano until there are no more keys, all twenty-four have been used up. If there was another key, E.J. Byrne would play its scale, the twenty-fifth state, but unfortunately there is no such thing.

Instead she swallows a tiny white bead, one of a decade prescribed for her unhappiness, should it arise – half of it, saving the other 2.5 milligrams for an hour later to make sure it is absolutely necessary (also that it will last until 11 pm).

E. has learned ecstasy

This is the Simplicity pattern for E.J. Byrne's happiness. She can use it over and over again, fitting the pieces on a size ten dummy, the size of a very small woman.

At first she thinks she must have a light body to achieve her most preferred state, the state of weightlessness (later she realizes it is not her body which has weightlessness among its possessions). She diets rigidly, living on Mogadon and the white wafers of the body of Christ.

She is not a great eater but her report card describes her as a high achiever and everyone is very pleased.

Music shop assistant (Wellington) knows a veil

In another age she would have been a jongleur. She spends her days demonstrating bamboo saxophones imported from Indonesia, but to no avail. The notes she plays carry no weight. ('They have no say-so la ti do,' says the frivolity of E.J. Byrne, amusing itself while she is not there, she is away in despair). The notes are gone before they can be sold. She has more success selling sheet music, a thin film noir.

A blackness (she does not see)

She tried to keep track of the beds she slept in and this was possible until the age of twenty-one. Now she has lost count – also of the dead people she knows, and she can no longer remember how each Christmas has been spent. It is quicker to count down. She reads a thermometer and keeps a chart to gauge the largest ovulation of her life, whether it has passed yet.

The paradox, according to E.J. Byrne, is that when you are young nothing happens, and that is precisely the time in your life when something happening is what you want most in the world. When you are older – just a little bit, the difference between one day, its close of trade, and the next – when you are quite capable of making things happen, they happen of their own volition.

The parallax is, there is nothing that does not match

She is drawn to women and she is drawn to men, but more so to the symmetry of herself drawn either way. She wears a dress with a line down the middle, black on one side, white on the other, forming herself in an image to attract likenesses. At all costs she must have one or the other.

She once went to a ball, 'Le blanc et le noir,' held on a public holiday in the foyer of a public library in New York City. To this she wore flaming red. A splash of colour in black and white will not be seen, as on a screen, thought E.J. Byrne. She dropped into bed on the vanishing line between night and day.

Falling for the cause of her weightlessness

A light flickering in a darkened room she has just entered, E.J. Byrne assumes it signifies a presence, and she genuflects, then looks round quickly, ready to explain it was just a slip of the knee. She sees the light comes from a television set. The image of a woman shines upon a man watching from a low chair opposite. Caught in the light between these two gazes, there is nothing E.J. Byrne can do, deflecting, but summon a great Passion for one of them.

A documentary about RSI

E.J. Byrne now believes this is what the women in her family have been suffering from – too many years all the same, an injurious action between Christmases. Following the advice of a television documentary, she turns her head to one side when serving customers in the music shop. She stands on tiptoe to prevent fallen arches, and rotates the wrist that once faced the sky. The coins in the palm of her hand fall to the floor.

A folk song at night
Die Lorelei, sung by a siren in a major key as it approaches, becomes minor once it has passed the fixed object, E.J. Byrne. If there was a key between major and minor, E.J. Byrne would play its scale, but there is no in-between.

A telephone rings few changes
A white telephone ringing in the middle of a dark night, a black one ringing in sunlight on a bright morning (an afternoon) – the voice E.J. Byrne answers with is the same for each, even though she knows one call announces; he turned his palm to the sky for a last injection of ecstasy; the other, the pharmaceutical firm offers a pall bearer. Why else does a telephone ring at these hours? As in dreams she knows the outcome but she does not know it. She is leaving this city.

Why E.J. Byrne can never leave
An angel fallen from a tombstone (life-size, the size of an angel or a four-year-old child) lost its arm and part of its wing under a bulldozer. A man she knew once found it and now it is her stability (it takes four people to lift it), also the reason she must leave.

What she does with her days still is sleep
They are throwing a little cutlery around the room. An 8 am start is the time they go to bed. They have reversed night and day, retrieving the outlines of sleeves, the inner circles of neckbands from the cutting-room floor. A length of film she makes use of for a false hem on a dress she once wore to a black and white ball – this to match the negatives she glimpses at the corners of her eyes when she is tired. Before she can get a proper look the negatives disappear. That is their nature. She suspects they may be the blackness of what is here (but she does not see).

Her bête noir is the thing she most desires
She is the mother of three pregnancy scares and that is more than enough.

'There is no need to bring any more blood tests into this world,' says E.J. Byrne.

Utopia seen from a distance

Once from the eleventh floor of a building in New York it was difficult for E.J. Byrne, drawn to the window, to identify a mass of falling objects. When she looked up they appeared to be part of a tickertape parade – looking down she saw the tiny flutter of pinstriped stockbrokers. The moment of her great sadness is also her happiness seen from above. She must have one or the other.

An injection calms her nerves

A Dystopia she once packed up and moved to by the picking of a fight, leaving soon afterwards for its opposite, a seduction. Now she need not search for these states, they fall into her lapdog. She takes an injection of passion at bedtime like a tablet with drawn eyelids. This is her bliss, the despair of which is a lover who once held her in the palm of her hand.

If she is wearing black, well, E.J. Byrne must wear white.

ANNABEL FAGAN

Coming Home

Billie dragged along the footpath with her family. How she hated
shopping, any sort of shopping, window-shopping in particular. What
ridiculous things they oohed and aahed over. The clothes were dreadful,
ten years, twenty years behind London and Europe. Call those
fashionable, she wanted to say, why they're vulgar, no taste, and . . .
far too bright. No class, no class at all in this swaggering little country
I was born in. Billie felt homesick for London, for a proper city where
the buildings had beauty and dignity, a sort of calmness about them
instead of here, where everything was new and edgy, even the people,
talk, talk, talking in that jarring New Zealand way.

They ambled, her mother, sister and the children, partly because her
mother was old and partly because they liked looking in every single
shop window. 'Mum, Mummy look. See Granny,' one of the children
was constantly calling. 'Yes dear, good heavens dear,' said Susan and
Mrs Snow patiently. So Billie had to amble too when all she wanted,
was to go quickly back to London or at least sit down somewhere and
have a decent cup of coffee. 'Look Billie, do you like that red skirt?'
said Susan. 'It'd suit you eh?' Billie wanted to cry. How badly they
spoke. New Zealanders seem incapable of opening their mouths – except
to eat and then they find it hard to close them again, judging by the
size of everyone. What a perfectly dreadful skirt. 'No,' she told her
sister, 'it's not my style at all.'

She wearily leaned against a lamp-post – a lamp-post! you'd think
it was the Wild West – while her mother and sister discussed last-minute
Christmas purchases. The window was full of useful, everyday gifts
– sets of tools for Dad, dinner-services for Mum, a wooden-backed
hairbrush for Dad, an ornate one with a soft, plump back for Mum.
'I need some tools so I can help Dad,' a wise child said. 'I'm going to
help Mum,' a wiser child said. 'If I had that pastry set I could, with
all those pretty shapes for biscuits, couldn't I Mum?' 'Wait and see what
Santa brings,' said Susan, smiling at her children, the apples of her

eye. 'Just wait and see, he might be listening now with his great big magic ears,' glancing at Mrs Snow. 'And his great big magic head and his great big magic eyes and his great big magic mouth, Santa, Santa,' shrieked the child, jumping up and down. Oh god, sighed Billie, why do they have to abbreviate everything. 'Santa Klaus,' she told the child, 'or Father Christmas, isn't that a nicer way of saying it, like a Daddy. Father Christmas,' she repeated tenderly. The child stopped jumping and regarded Billie with scorn. 'He can't be a Daddy, he hasn't got a wife. And he's even old, very, very, very old. He's not a father, he's an old, old Santa.'

Billie felt humiliated. She felt her sister should reprimand the children. She was sure they wanted to shout, '*Billie you're so silly*.' They didn't respect her, not that she cared. New Zealand children were dreadfully young for their ages and couldn't articulate very well. They mumbled and said 'eh' and were big and brown. They didn't wear shoes, only those terrible jandals or nothing and their feet looked dirty and tough. Feet were ugly and their naked shapes reminded her of creepie-crawlie sinister things, which by themselves could creep across the floor and crawl, repulsive and slimy, all over her clean skin, writhing around her arms and legs and digging at her with their toe-nails. Feet should be kept under something, held down, hidden away, under the sink, yes, with all those other murky objects and tied to the waste-pipe so they couldn't escape.

Billie nodded to herself. She felt better.

Mrs Snow and Susan disappeared into the shop. 'Stay outside,' they said, 'stay with Aunty Billie.' 'Not Aunty, just call me Billie,' she told them. 'But you are our Aunty,' the boy said. 'My name's Billie not Aunty,' she explained. 'I like to be called by my name, just as I call you by your names, not niece and nephew.' 'Dad calls me Son,' the child said. 'I don't call my Mummy Susan or my Dad Stew,' the girl said. 'Children don't call grown-ups by their names when the children are only little. We don't call you just Billie. In any case it's a boy's name,' she said. 'A little boy's name,' said the boy.

Billie turned from the children and watched the people – men in shorts, women in shorts, in a city! Crowds of them with skin over-exposed to the sun. They should be more careful. Susan gardened a great deal. She smiled when Billie mentioned the ill-effects of the sun – wrinkles, aging and cancer.' 'I know, I know,' she said, 'I must remember to wear a hat. But I love to feel the sun, it warms me right through to my bones. And my garden, I can't neglect my garden, look at those ferns uncurling. Look Billie. They like the sun too. We all of us live and then die, eh.'

Billie felt ashamed for New Zealanders. For her sister in clothes that didn't suit her, for the children in their jandals, for her mother in that flowery dress and plastic beads, and her hair so obviously permed, why couldn't it look more natural? She had been back in this country for two months and she hated and despised the place. And who wouldn't after living for three years in a cultured environment full of decent music and theatre and civilized people. In comparison, New Zealanders were so insular – where are their minds? she wondered. Mrs Snow and Susan emerged from the shop. 'What'd you get, what'd you get,' clamoured the children. 'Let's look for ice-creams,' answered Susan. 'And a cup of tea,' said Mrs Snow.

In the cafe Billie saw how tired her mother was, god she was tired herself. She also noticed how scruffy the blue beads were, how can she wear such rubbish. The children sucked and puffed at their milkshakes while Susan made tiny rasping sighs after every few sips of her pale tea. Billie, as she drank her boiled coffee, tried not to count the sips between the sighs, one or two. She noticed her mother not touching her tea but studying it with enjoyment and satisfaction, as if that was enough, she didn't need to drink, just looking seemed to sate her, made her shoulders unclench and caused the crumpled flowers on her dress to stretch out in blossom. She took a sip, 'Ahhhh,' she said. Poor old thing, I'll buy her some nice new beads, thought Billie.

After several starts they were off, recharged and refreshed, the children by a last-minute pie each with tomato sauce, Susan by an egg sandwich, Mrs Snow by 'that small cake at the end dear, the one with jam on top of the cream, I love raspberry jam,' and Billie by her quest.

She popped into the first trinket shop they came to without telling the others. It won't take long, I want them to be a surprise, she thought, tons of necklaces to choose from. She picked one out immediately, the first that was pretty. The beads were flowers like forget-me-nots, blue and white petals, open and touching in the summer air. 'Pretty, eh?' asked the assistant.

'Oh, they're lovely,' said Billie. 'They're china, aren't they? I'll have them.'

'Plastic,' answered the assistant. 'These are china. You can't tell the difference, can you, except by the price. Of course if you want a really special present, the quality of these is superior . . .'

'I've already bought my mother a Christmas present, in England.

I just . . . want a gift, a little extra present you know, not too expensive.'

'Well, they definitely look like china,' said the assistant. 'They're made out of a new type of plastic which doesn't resemble plastic at all.' She held them up. 'See how they shine.'

'Well, they don't look like plastic . . .' Billie touched them, 'They don't feel like plastic . . .'

'You can't tell they're plastic, no way. I've got some my friend thinks are china and I wouldn't tell her any different, except if she asked me.'

The assistant smiled at Billie. What a nice woman, Billie thought. 'I'll have them,' she said. She was pleased with herself for being so decisive, for finding such pretty beads and china ones at that, well almost. I'm sure this plastic has china components, it couldn't shine like that otherwise. And they were her mother's favourite colour, blue. I could have got her a nice change, red, but of course that's my favourite colour. She laughed at herself and thought excitely, I'll give them to her now and get rid of those other ghastly things. She'll be glad to throw them away, thrilled to have elegant new beads instead. How thoughtful of you dear, she'll say, how kind, you shouldn't have spent so much money. Would you mind disposing of these old things for me, they've had their day. It's nothing, nothing, Billie would answer, don't you worry about the price, Mother, I've been intending to get a job soon.

Her family were waiting patiently outside, shuffling slightly, leaning into one another like a little mob of sheep. 'There you are,' they said.

'I've bought you a present, Mum, Mother.'

'Have you dear,' said Mrs Snow tiredly.

'Where's ours, have you got one for us too?' asked the children.

'No,' said Billie.

'Have you got one for our Mummy?'

'No,' said Billie, giving the gift to her mother. 'Only for Granny, she's tired.'

'We're tired too,' said the children.

'Dear, dear,' said Mrs Snow, moving her parcels around. 'You can help me open it in the car,' she told them, 'we're going home now. Come on. Off we go.'

'Oh Mother, please open it now,' Billie said. 'Oh please. The car's miles away.'

Mrs Snow looked at her daughter. 'All right,' she said, 'hold my parcels dear.' The beads almost fell out of the bag on to the footpath. 'Careful,' said Billie, 'they're china, they'll break.' Mrs Snow beamed. 'Billie dear, they're lovely, so pretty don't you think Susan, look children, my favourite colour, I'll wear them for Christmas.' 'Wear them now,' said Billie, and tumbling her parcels to the ground, slipped behind her mother and quickly popped off the old beads, noticing with distaste that each one was encircled by a faint discolouration like pale dirt. She pushed them into her bag and took the forget-me-not flowers from her mother's hands. 'There,' she said. 'Look how beautiful the new beads are, much better. Much, much better, Susan?' Mrs Snow peered at herself in the shop window. 'Yes, they are, they'll be for best.' 'Lovely Mum,' said Susan, 'now help Billie with the parcels you kids, home-time!'

Billie hung back for a moment and dropped the old beads into a rubbish-bin. She won't be wearing those grubby things again.

In the car Mrs Snow settled herself and the children in the back while Billie sat in the front with Susan. Mrs Snow rustled around. 'Just a minute Susan, I must put my beads back on and keep these for Christmas. There. Can I have them Billie? Very kind of you dear. A pretty gift.'

Billie felt cold and clammy in the warm car. She swung around to her mother. 'Oh I threw those old things away,' she said. 'I didn't think you needed them any more, I thought you meant me to get rid of them for you.' She felt Susan looking at her and heard a sound from her sister like a slap. The children were silent. 'I mean,' said Billie, 'I bought them because of that, because you didn't want the old ones, they were had-it and worn, that's why . . . I . . .' Mrs Snow was looking at her daughter. Her face was tired and sad, her hands lay still in her lap.

'Wait,' said Billie. She got out of the car and started to run back along the footpath but the shoppers got in her way and she couldn't hurry. She stumbled from lamp-post to lamp-post, from bin to bin but the beads weren't there. Oh god, oh god, they've gone. She felt they were in her throat choking her. She wanted to sink down and cry. She wanted to curl into the footpath and be unrecognizable.

She searched for the next bin, and . . . There they were, she could see them! Bright and blue, sitting in the sun on top of all the rubbish, just as she'd left them. Whoosh, she breathed.

Billie climbed into the car. 'Here you are,' she said. She felt absolved. Wear them then, she thought, they're yours. Put the bloody things back on, and see if I care.

Mrs Snow fastened the beads around her neck. 'Thank you dear,' was all she said. But there was just a little bit of malice in the way she said it.

TERRY DRIESSEN

Curious Perspective

Easter 1986 and four days' holiday. Holy-days, her mother called them, revealing her foreign-ness in this, and other linguistic oddities. Time to watch the grass grow, which it certainly had while she'd been away, and to let the mind wander, which it would anyway. Really the grass was beyond a joke, rampant over what in summer had been the tomatoes, and making the concrete slabs to the clothes-line a damp and treacherous causeway. If she were not so tired, if her body were not glued, possibly permanently, to the step she sat on, she could have dealt with the back lawn situation. As it was, rather than she felling it, the grass threatened to engulf her. Already she saw it, the yellow fetid blades of undergrowth, slugs and snails swollen to enormous size, her shrunken self greeting a curious ant, Take me to your leader.

Four days out. The hospital was in some respects meticulous about time, counting it like pills, and on Holy Thursday at 5 pm they had handed her a little bundle of these in packages labelled A.M., Midday, P.M. and For Emergencies. These gestures to order were a comfort to the insane, who rightly perceived that they were invaded by disorder.

Stuff pills into overnight bag. Elaborate disregard: I will take them if I remember. Wash them down with brandy, of which there will surely be a not-yet-finished bottle at home. I will take them because they induce vivid dreams and because, chemically speaking, I am careless of my body. A bio-chemical minefield: watch this space. Try vitamins and achieve new dynamism.

I remember shoes, and return to my room. Stuff these too into overnight bag. Not a room, really it is a cell, and I can keep it neat as any since belongings here are not an issue. Starched white sheets, pale blue bedspread with hospital corners tucked in, mattress on the floor. Suitably sobering. A row of things, also on the floor, including flowers, a bunch of these in a vase managing to look calculatedly dishevelled. Dear Jay. The things you think of. I would have forgotten the transistor I see now, a live thing on the bed and in the throes of 'Stabat Mater'. This also very suitable, and nearly quadrophonic with these walls.

Not to go yet. The radio across the corridor belts out a Beatles song. Funny, the unexpected in some people. He's a tough cookie, a Maori with tattoos, a swastika on the back of one hand. Yesterday, a few days ago, you were Bruno Lawrence, the last man on earth, and I was your princess. Will you dance, thank you kind sir. It's evaporating now. Another time, another place, Mark came to visit: I am a grandmother, my cat has six kittens. Very muddling. The ward cat wanders past, doubles back and stops outside my cell. Tiger burning bright. Not exactly. Well-fed. What had they done with the kittens? Drowned, most likely. Six little corpses. Try to remember. They might have gone to the farm. Plenty of room to run about and multiply.

Time to go. The male nurse with dark-tinted spectacles, polychromatic, has stopped outside, sees I'm still here. Light-sensitive eyes. A real hood. For four days and nights of wildly elastic and subjective time my incarcerator, a member of the Gestapo's thought police. This one brought me meals on trays. Unbolted the door leaving reinforcements, shadows I could see in the fluorescent light of the corridor outside. While he was there I could sit on my mattress, watch his calves in black trousers. These boots are made for kicking if I make a break for it he will. I eat and drink soberly, polish it off with a smoke. Polite reminder: don't ask for a second to keep you going as a refusal often offends. Tread softly. Someone has left cigarette burns on the insides of my arms. Could it be me? I do another one while I have the opportunity. Just testing. Why don't I feel it? Smell of scorched flesh. I mean to say, it's scars on the soul we are counting. I do another one for good measure. As good a hood as any other, I wear my scars with arrogance. Little enough in this world to be proud of. He has picked up the tray and gone, bolting the door again. I ate and drank in darkness and silence. We all need a break, and I needed the rest. As they leave they turn on the microphones and the tape-recorder. I am under observation again and must begin walking and talking, talking all the time for the microphones. But I am so tired of walking day and night, night and day, and my feet are so sore. I sing a song, 'It's a long way to Tipperary'. My head needs the break too. The Experimenters.

Pick up overnight bag. It has been around and is cunningly disguised as a sports bag. I pass through the ward and see its other inmates busily and noisily engaged in meal-time. Hence the quietness in the cell-block. Engaged in eating, their numbers depleted due to the holiday weekend, both they and the departing I appear not to belong here. The hospital as a hotel, a cheap holiday for housewives. Try to think of it as a rest-cure, they said to me once, lots of people do. I put up a fight, to prevent who? from becoming complacent.

Doreen, the transsexual, is in the lounge. She stops me for a light. She and the big woman, Marj, both have slash scars all the way up their arms. Doreen is in bandages again today. She lights her smoke from mine. Perfect peace. I love this woman too, for the time being, and the clothes she wears, the result of a forty-eight hour shopping spree. Unlike me, she goes for second-hand, but *glamorous*. Budgeted extravagance.

I am leaving. The door's unlocked for a wonder. There could be a code I have not yet deciphered to the lock/unlocked-ness of doors. Time-lapse security. I sing another song, for myself this time. If I only had time.

This has to be the best time of day, of year. Afternoon falling into evening. Cease from striving. I conceal this holiday carelessness. Headbent, itinerant, I am an old man. Existing shiftlessly, I sleep under bridges. Pack up my troubles. The Samoan bus-driver seems overwhelmingly kind. I have the correct change ready and he puts it painstakingly in the correct box. All in five-cent pieces, do I save them up on purpose? Happy accident. The city is crowded, shoppers bustle and stroll. I become a human being carrying an overnight bag and head for Woolworths where I buy four yellow furry Easter chickens, seven small hard eggs, and a roll of sellotape. Outside, I take out two of the chicks, two of the eggs, stick up the rest in the bag and sellotape on the addressed envelope I have brought with me. This parcel will wing its way via the next red letter-box and the courtesy of the Post Office (no stamp) to its I hope grateful recipient, perhaps making it in time for Easter Sunday. Ritual.

I drift, savouring the Hare Krishnas, the posters celebrating occurrences past and to come. Enough happening. Then up Victoria Street. Bottles, brandy and wine. A moderate imbiber and for visitors.

I should detour to the church: Bless me father for I have sinned. Unspecific on detail, specific on times. For verisimilitude. Do all children invent sins because they have forgotten? Father, I knew not what I did. Nothing to forgive. A faultless society, it knew no transgression. Perfect crime.

Lutte pour l'abolition de la torture et de la peine de mort.

Australian hospitals have the edge. I consider myself a connoisseur of cruelty. Head bent, I traverse the intersection. Screech of car brakes. Your life in your hands. I step with care over the cracks in the footpath. An Australian hospital could keep a body forever. Forever stretches, an eternity of mornings with blank faces. Twice weekly a brace of doctors comes to my bed. They wear white coats, their faces have no expression, and except that one has a beard they might be twins. They ask how I am today. No better it appears, and they still don't think me ready to leave just yet. My behaviour is not appropriate. I search my mind for behaviour suitable for this place. I decline to explain the absolute reasonableness of dropping yesterday's dinner on the floor. Crash of breaking crockery. Bedlam, then time in solitary, following the action/reaction principle. With – I think – admirable institutional detachment I bring up the subject of air-conditioning. The climate, I say. I am chairman of a committee and may dispose of funds within reasonable bounds. They too, it appears, are all for it. In a clatter of keys they depart securely. This summer heat twelve months ago. I see another year of ward meal-times stretching, seasonally adjusted and not ignoring ward morning and afternoon tea-times. Doubled in bulk. I attempt youthful voluptuousness. I admire the Spanish lady in the bed next to me. Her lover brings her Roses chocolates which she eats steadily, without greed. She is pleased with herself and smiles, through her black eyes, slowly.

After a long time I am taken to the swimming pool. The water is bright blue, and sparkles; it is crowded, and the voices have a different quality in this stretch of air. I sink like a stone, and wish I was lying on my bed, and safe within four walls with people who are as large as I am.

A long time ago there was a boy with fair hair. Together, yogic-ly, we saluted the sun. Now there is a girl, Frances, with long hair, and she makes me listen to a song. So high that I might almost see eternity.

Somewhere there is a straight line stretching from here to the sky. My desk is not cluttered as it usually is, but neat, and the drawers also, tidy, so that anything I need I am able to find immediately.

Outside, the grass is not rampant, but tended. A figure, small as a boy, dark-haired, gumbooted and woollen for the approaching winter, kneels bent over the ground under the oak tree in the far corner. She loosens the earth with her trowel, planting bulbs, carefully haphazard. Inside in the kitchen, which is clean and swept, there is a circular polished oak table and on the table four fluffy yellow Easter chicks and five small, hard chocolate eggs.

ARAPERA HINEIRA

Innocence of Sin

Wawata was waiting for the bus, like everyone else, delaying going home to the smell of cow shit and yelling parents. She leaned against the shop verandah post, carved by those who loved, or dreamed of loving, some parts worn to a shiny brown by horses and people rubbing their buttocks.

The half-red half-yellow ancient bus finally clanked to a halt right in front of Wawata. The waiting kids danced and screeched.
   Ya ya! Ugly hakari bus! Ugly hakari bus!
   He did that on purpose!
   What!
   That bloody tin-leg bus driver. Nearly ran over my feet!
   Wawata shot up from under, grabbing the soles of her feet.
   You made me skid you peg-leg!
   If you had two legs like my gammy one you won't feel nothing.
Kaitoa! Sit somewhere else. This is a bus stop!

The high school kids piled out. The new girl was first off followed by at least six heavies.
   Wawata watched longingly.

'Neat figure ne Wawata.
   Not bad. Skirt too short. I can see her pants.
   Yeah that's what they're after. Kaore e roa. Won't be long!
   No it won't. Know what my brother said? She's only been here two weeks and guess what. She's already started leaving her window open at night.
   Wawata sighed.
   Yeah that's bad. Asking for it.
   The six heavy hopefuls swaggered behind, down her road. The dancing and screeching started again.

Ya ya ya you going the wrong way.

One big heavy about-turned, clenching his fist.

I'll kick your bloody arses.

The chanting continued, the kids knowing no harm would come to them. The bold ones played follow-the-leader behind the heavies. The rest picked up the mail and the bread and scattered home.

Wawata's teacher appeared, just as the bus rattled off, unlocked his bicycle from the fence, and wheeled it round almost on to her feet, just as she stepped on to the gravel with the mail and the bread. He grinned. She looked down suddenly shy. He made girls feel like that!

Gidday Wawata. Edged his front wheel closer. Gee you're getting big.

As if he didn't know!

Looking good too.

She kicked the front wheel. God it hurt. Sweat pin-pricked. Hot feelings stirred. She fled home.

Wawata changed into her milking clothes, put on her gumboots, reached the cowshed dreaming of being a new girl.

You're late. Wasting time at the shop again. Her brother went on. Hanging around the shop is kid's stuff. You're getting too old for that. You want to watch out for those high school boys. They think they're shit hot!

Wawata cut in on him. You know what. They're all after that new girl. She think's she's shit hot too.

Rua responded. They got no show. I know. I hear everything in the pub. They're not the only rams round here!

Her father appeared. The talking stopped. He too nagged about her lateness.

Come straight home. No need for you to collect the mail and the bread. Leave it to the young ones. Last summer it was reading in the cream stand. Now it's dawdling somewhere else. Next year it's boarding school for you girl. No distractions there!

He always spoilt things. Just when Rua was treating her like a grown-up he had to talk about boarding school. She hosed out the cow muck. She couldn't wait until the milking finished.

You know what Rua? You should go somewhere else to work. Dad treats us all the same. He's scared of us growing up.

Nah. I'm all right. He doesn't mind if I go to the pub. Engari koe. Girls are different. They get pregnant. That's where that new girl should be too. In that school you're going to. No chance to muck around there!

Milking over, they plodded home, Wawata musing.
   It's a wonder they're not scared of the dog.
   What dog?
   That Pakeha's. The new girl's dad.
   That's not her dad. She's Maori all over.
   He is her dad! He adopted her.
   Oh yeah. That's right. Hmmm! Probably a mean little runt like the
owner. Ask your mate if it bites. She should know. She takes them
milk every morning.
   Course it does. And yaps! It's a fox terrier.
   Hmmm. I'll choke the runt if it picks on me. Rua's boot swung out
as though kicking for goal.
   You like her too don't you? Wawata asked, suddenly suspicious there
was more action than the pub talk.
   Not me but I know one bull who does. And he's bloody well married.
That bastard gets away with it!
   Wawata pretended she knew. She pounced on a name. But Rua
wouldn't say. He enjoyed leading her on.
   A voice boomed out. Hey. Kua reri nga kai! Hurry up before the
food gets cold!

Slurping sounds. Scraping plates. Scrumptious dinner. Wawata drying
dishes. Older sister washing up. Her turn to gossip.
   You know what? There's a new girl here!
   She's not new. She's two weeks old!
   Smartie. You know what I mean. She's pinched my boyfriend.
   Aw! That's why you're still here. You told Mum you got a job lined
up in Wellington. I bet there's plenty neat ones down there.
   Don't want to talk about Wellington. Don't want you getting your
head full of sex. You're too young. So is she. Only fifteen! I'm eighteen.
And I've finished school!

What a waste of time talking to older brother and sister. Never really
said too much about you-know-what. Not like her mate. Didn't mind
what they talked about.

You know what Manawanui, good of that Pakeha to adopt her. Fancy
going all over the country with a black kid. What's her name?

Mahiti. She's a darkie all right. Bet they didn't do it for aroha. More like they wanted a servant for nothing. She's from the welfare. Those kids get hell from some of our own. It must be worse with a Pakeha!

Don't think so. Tell you what. She's got lovely dresses. And she's allowed to go to the pictures on her own. Neat eh! Dad won't let me.

It wasn't long before the new year arrived. So did the anticipated misery of boarding school. First month terrible. Rules, regulations, etiquette. Prayer before breakfast and dinner. School not bad. Six book shelves of leather-bound volumes of Dickens, Shakespeare, Thackeray, Wordsworth, Tennyson, bequeathed to the school by its literary patrons. Marvellous stuff if you knew how.

Older sister made her way to Wellington. Hoha from playing the dignified whaiaipo, but kept the bush telegraph operating. At long last she broke the silence of the unrepeatable, though not without a little drama.

Wawata was called into the principal's office.

Sit down little one. I have a letter here from your sister. I do not approve of its contents, and neither will your parents. I will let you have it because we in this church school believe in making our students feel at home by keeping in touch with their families. But it is my Christian duty to tell you that we do not condone swearing, whether orally or in writing – waving the filthy epistle as though to purify the air – and we do not approve of mentioning the misfortunes of the fallen!

Wawata stared at her shoes. Yes Miss White. I'm sorry. I'll tell her not to say dirty things – inwardly busting to get her hands on the juicy letter.

She felt a lump in her throat. Swallowed hard to stop from crying.

Well here you are, said Miss White in gentler tones. It's my duty to say these things. Write to her on Sunday and show me your reply.

Wawata stumbled out clutching her letter.

Dear Wawata,

Settling down in the big smoke. I miss Mum's yelling and Dad's preaching. But I don't miss you know who! You might be snotty-nosed but you were quite right. This place is neat. I've joined a basketball team. We play in the mornings on Saturday and watch rugby in the afternoons. We follow a neat rugby team. And I've met this really big,

*big handsome Maori from the South Island. Doesn't talk Maori at all.
They don't down there. Tell you what though, he talks real good
English. Not like at home, half-Maori half-Pakeha. We all belong to
this neat Maori club and we're raising money for a new marae in the
Hutt. Saturdays and Sundays are just great. Sports, then the pub with
the boys, then to the Club to eat pork bones and puha and takakau.
Then the rest of the evening for you-know-what. That's all you get.
Ha! Ha! Ha! My big secret.*

*Guess what's happening up home. You know that girl Mahiti? Well
she doesn't mahiti now. She's too hapu. And I say kaitoa for pinching
my boyfriend. But I'll say this much for the pokokohua. It wasn't him!
It was guess who! That ram of a school teacher of yours. I hope that
baby is blacker and uglier than he is, the randy bee! You know what,
that Pakeha father of hers made him sign a paper that it is his baby?
It isn't even born yet! But I still hope it's his. They've sent her away
the poor kid. Up north somewhere. All bullshit if you ask me! Every
cow and bull knows anyway. Your aunties and your mother are really
going on about it. 'Ka mau te wehi' from one house to the next, the
hypocrites. I bet they even carry on gossiping after the ten
commandments and all that on Sundays.*

*Never mind kiddo. You keep yourself good and clean in your mind.
You can't get hapu that way.*

Arohanui,

From your one-and-only big, big sister.

*P.S. Don't tell Dad I'm going to the pub and don't tell Mum I've got
a boyfriend. Don't want her kehuas spying on me!*

Dear Manawanui,

*Thanks a lot for your letter. I hope you are having a really good
time and looking after yourself.*

*I really like this school. We have a lovely principal. She is a good
Christian lady with a gentle voice. She's always wearing lovely clothes.
I've made lots of lovely friends, mostly from up home. Some of them
are really clever. We read a lot of Shakespeare on wet Saturdays. We're
going to start up a drama club. Stops us from getting into mischief.*

*There's not much news around here but I have to tell you that my
principal says you mustn't write swear words or tell me the home gossip.
She says you shouldn't write about the misfortunes of others.*

*Must sign off now. Please send me some lollies and fruit. We are
allowed to have them.*

> *Arohanui,*
> *God bless you,*
> *From your little sister.*
P.S. *Parekareka ki a au o korero. Kei te koingo atu hoki ki te wakainga.*

The letter passed inspection. A brief polite reply arrived, two months later. 'Expect a parcel of goodies' cheered Wawata up immensely. She had expected silence. Now she couldn't wait. It arrived on a late spring afternoon. The goodies were unwrapped in front of the principal. There was no note. She and her friends feasted at midnight on chocolates wrapped in gold paper. Sheer heaven!

Here, Wawata whispered to her best mate. You have the box for your hankies.

Gee thanks, Wawata. It's really pretty.

Wawata sat in the classroom, dreaming of Christmas and her sister in Wellington. Her desk mate nudged her.

You're lucky you got me for a true honest friend. You know what was at the bottom of that box? Here! She shoved ten dollars wrapped in a letter over to Wawata. Lucky beast!

Dear Wawata,

Hope you really enjoy this parcel kiddo. Best way to collect mates. Just like us back home hanging around those kids with the best lunches. You've got some jail-house there. Fancy reading your letters. You poor kid! But at least you didn't get strapped all because of my big trap. You know what I think? It's all rupahu about Christian duty and all that. They are just all ihu those Christian ladies. And I bet she's never had a man! They're usually maroke types who are in charge of those Church schools. No sense of humour. No aroha. Karakia, karakia, karakia, all the time. Just like our father. Mind you, you can't call him maroke with all of us kids running around tutu haere ana!

I'm busting to tell you they were all wrong up home. The bush telegraph did it this time! Guess-a-thousand-times-who-the-father's-baby is?

To go back to the beginning. You know where Mahiti had her baby? In the maternity home near Auckland where our Aunty Kere is nursing. Well she helped to deliver Mahiti's baby. Take that! What a small world! And I won't keep you guessing any longer than I have to. The baby is not your black teacher's. IT HAS GOT REAL BLUE EYES!

And guess what else! Your teacher lost his job. And that pokokohua Pakeha father of Mahiti has sold his garage and gone up north too!

See you Christmas time. Sorry I said those awful things about Mahiti. I've really fallen for my big big man.

> *Look after yourself,*
> *Arohanui and lots of kisses,*
> *From your one-and-only big, big sister.*

hapu − pregnant

hoha − sick of, fed up

kaitoa − serves you right

mahiti − to jump

maroke − dry

pokokohua − boiled head

tutu haere ana − fooling about

whaiaipo − lower

NGAHUIA TE AWEKOTUKU

The Basketball Girls

Tihi looked at herself in the mirror. Closely, critically. Decided she
was ready to go out into the kitchen and show herself off to the family
– Koro and the kids, maybe an auntie or two or three, having a cup
of tea and warming their feet by the coal range.

Everyone – everything – stopped as she came through the door. Tall,
fair, and slim. She let them all inspect her; she was proud of her long
shapely legs in the sheer black stockings (two and eleven from Matthias,
what a bargain eh), her firm supple knees (she was too quick to fall,
and much too vain to graze them on the knotty asphalt court); and
her flexibly fine ankles cased in the black canvas boots. Tihi was a
Basketball Girl. And she was one of the best.

And oh, how I loved to look at her. Saturday afternoons that winter,
off I'd rush next door, straight after breakfast, quick as whitebait, into
Koro's kitchen to ogle and admire. Staring at Tihi was a treat. And
following her from a safe distance was even more of a treat, as long
as we didn't 'cramp my style, you kids'.

She'd meet her mates at the Hindu shop. Two of them, Cindy and
Pera. And they'd buy soft drinks in slender glass bottles, with long wax
pink straws. Green River, they'd say. Matching the colour of our girdles
and ties. Green River – for luck.

Meanwhile, we'd all be hanging back – if there was a gang of us
– and we'd wait for the bottles, which were dropped more or less in
the same place every time. One with a chewed straw (Pera), one with
the straw rammed and buckled in the bottle (Cindy), and one still neat
and whole (Tihi). Each bottle was worth fourpence. Three made a
shilling. Wow, that was a fortune!

Which I never made, for I was too busy watching Tihi. She walked
like a princess. Very straight, yet there was a ripple in there too. Maybe
like a panther, with her long black legs. Her gym was always pressed
and almost sharp at the edges of every one of her six box pleats – three
in front, and three at the back, that made twelve edges. Done early

every Saturday morning, with the iron hot from the range; and a well-scrubbed, damp, worn out flour bag with the edges picked out. Every pleat was just right; so that the gym hung from her shoulders like a straight black box, with big sections in it, like panels. Over a snowy white long-sleeved blouse, with a specially stiffened collar. And a carefully knotted emerald green tie. Koro himself taught Tihi how to do the tie up 'tika' – properly; and he was truly pleased with himself that day, folding the green silk fabric in his barky old fingers, chuckling at his attentive mokopuna. Tihi. Te Tihi Teitei o Kahukura. The highest arch of Kahukura; Rainbow's End. She was well named. And she showed how well she'd learned to do the tie, by skilfully knotting the girdle as well. The colour of new spring grass, woven into a length of narrow wool, two yards long, cutting the box pleats in half, nipping into her waist, lifting the hem even shorter! This always interested me – the gym no longer looked like a big black box; it pulled out very slightly over Tihi's chest, while still going straight down the back, though all the pleats gathered and crimped, just a little way over the girdle, and fell in a skirt to the middle of her thighs.

Underneath the hem were other things too; they popped and snapped and kept the black stockings up, pulling taut an inky black line that ran from her heel all the way up the back of her leg. Cindy, Pera, and Tihi spent a lot of time worrying about these lines – those damn seams they were called, as the three twirled and danced and twisted, craning their necks over their shoulders, peering down at the back of their knees. Pera had the most trouble; she was shorter, but somehow much fuller, and though she ironed her gym just like Tihi, it just flared and flounced, swelling out in the front at the top, and jutting like a shelf from the back of her bum. So her hem was sort of even.

Tihi always made sure her damn seams were straight. 'Cos that's a *rule*', Pera would roll the words out, husky and rich, and they'd laugh and laugh. Even Cindy, who seemed a bit sour, she'd laugh in a gravelly, raw-voiced way. Her knees were always grazed, her eyes were always there, on Tihi. They would shine like dark embers from her strong face; though not the prettiest, she was the tallest in their trio. And she starred on the basketball court, shot after shot after shot.

Off down the street they'd stride, arms linked, Tihi in the middle, Pera on the right, Cindy on the left, all in rhythm. The Basketball Girls. Pleased with the world, and with each other. Going to meet their mates. Going to play the game. Going to win.

Saturday after Saturday, I followed them, and I wondered at their pride, and their grace, and their beauty. Even on wet days, when the rain lashed the asphalt like acid, and their boots would slide and slip, their pony tails flop and straggle. Even on days when they got 'cleaned up', usually by a visiting team from a bigger town – because at home, they knew they were the best. They had the trophies to prove it. And Auntie Lily, with her green lapels lined with a brazen glitter of badges, she said so. She was the coach, and a ref, and the selector, and she knew. That was that.

So spring came, and all the skinny willow trees turned the colour of the river, and the season was over. No more basketball till next year. No more following Tihi and her mates down the street on a Saturday afternoon. No more till next year.

And eventually, next year, winter, arrived. After a summer of blinding white softball pants and Tihi with a sunburned nose and cracked mouth and peroxide streak in her hair. Which was still in a ponytail, with the same green ribbon.

Winter arrived. And with it came Ahi. In a gleaming two-toned Zephyr Six, with bright red stars that flashed like rubies on the fenders. Ahi turned up to take Tihi to basketball, every Saturday. Just Tihi, because Pera had moved to the coast to look after her Kuia, and Cindy – well, she had just sort of vanished. Dropped out of sight. Who knew where.

Still young, still nosey, I'd hang around next door while Tihi got ready for the game. She still had that magic for me, even though she didn't meet her two mates any more at the Hindu shop; and with no Green River bottles to fight over, the other kids weren't interested in staying around. Tihi would meet Ahi instead; Ahi, who pulled up in the gateway in that amazing car. Ahi, with thick, jet black hair cut like Elvis but a little longer at the back, like a fat duckbum. And dark glasses, green green glass in thick plastic frames. Ahi, who never smiled . . . and never got out of the car to go in and meet Koro either. Just waited, quietly, then revved the motor as Tihi gaily pranced out, flipped open the passenger door, kissed Ahi on the cheek, and then with a filmstar wave at her greatest fan (me) was off. Down the road with Ahi, who somehow felt familiar to me. Somehow.

Then it happened. Koro had a turn one Saturday morning, just as Tihi was ironing the sleeves of her blouse. She rushed out the door and was back in five minutes with Auntie Nel who had a car and worked

at the hospital. They took Koro up there, where he was to stay and
get fussed over for a couple of weeks.

And I was told to wait, and tell Ahi.

Oh, I thought, my eleven-year-old brain buzzing with the
responsibility, my face a smear of tears. What was I going to say?

The car pulled up, all polished and shining. Ahi was checking the
dark glasses in the rear-vision mirror. Slowly, I walked over, carefully
arranging my story. It still came out all garbled though; but Ahi got
the message, while I blubbered on pitifully.

The car door opened, and Ahi got out, kneeled down, still not saying
a word. One strong arm went around me. I stopped snivelling, leaned
into the black satin shirt of Tihi's hero, Ahi. Who took off the dark
glasses, and looked at me. Smiling, talking softly in a voice I *knew*!

'Don't worry, Huri girl, Koro will be fine, you'll see.'

It was Cindy. Ahi had Cindy's eyes, and Cindy's voice. Cindy had
come back as Ahi. Wow! It felt like a secret – it felt neat, though!
I was dying to run away and tell someone.

But I didn't. I just went to church and to youth club and to school
and waited for Saturday mornings. And the magic of Tihi, getting ready
for the game, getting ready for Ahi.

Getting ready for us.

RAWINIA WHITE

The Return

I reached the T intersection 'Matahina 16 km/Te Teko 5 km' and parked in front of the gate. 'NO TRESPASSERS – TRESPASSERS WILL BE PROSECUTED'. There were a Mitsubishi van and people outside the nearby house.

I stood, my inner-being still ignoring my denial of being Maori, my decision at an intellectual level that I must be Pakeha. Yet there was always a knowing, a calling of something else, and the calls were becoming louder and louder and stronger and stronger to the part inside of me that could hear.

The sign said, '*NO*! Don't walk on this land. Do as you are told! The past is the past!'

And the calling was a karanga from the people who had walked that land before me and I no different from all the others who had become Pakeha, except for a something in me that had a knowing, that still had ears.

But your mother is not Maori, she has no language, she has no whanaunga Maori, and many, many New Zealanders have a little Maori blood. You're no different. Just get on with it, forget!

I have walked this tight rope all my life.

Last time, in early January, I stepped back from the gate and looked over the hot moving tar into the shimmering body of the land, the blue/purple shaded mountain vivid against the bright blue sky. I remember looking towards the house, along the line of blackberries, red and black fruit hanging, that fringed the body of the land. But I did not get over the gate then. Now still the mountain stands above the gate and the sign, with the same quiet knowing that is without words yet speaks with a stirring and sighing from within itself to that within me becoming a pull towards the land.

But, now, where is my way to begin to tell you how I feel? How can I start? I come alone, there is only me. I stand whakama because

I know I cannot say your name as it should be said yet with a new shame I cannot say Mt Edgecumbe is your name. I bring with me the sorrow for all that has happened. My mother knew about this place, she grew up Pakeha, but carried a secret inside herself. We have been Pakeha ever since, but still, a something, a something that has brought me here and back now again to talk to you. Kaore he nui taku reo, engari he mihi nui ki a koutou katoa.

And the words she was trying to find turned to what she had been taught of the reo of those who had been, and seemed to be gone from her, into the language that is beyond words and cannot be written. Out of this beginning emerged the reason why a woman would come so far to stand alone on a remote country road to talk out loud and stare into a space where there *is* no one, *is* there?

Leaning against the fence outside the house was a koroua.

'My mother has some shares in this land, can I go for a walk on it?'

'Course, well if it's your mother's land, what are you asking me for? If you get lost in the maize sing out. Who's your mother, is she a Hayes, or is she a Keepa . . .?'

SUE REIDY

Dog Boy

The dog boy is wailing again. A lonely ribbon of sound which winds through the night.

For once, I can experience some empathy with him.

I feel like joining him in his kennel. I could do some howling myself. The two of us together – baying at the full moon.

But finally, the dog boy's mother takes him into the house.

The neighbours will be relieved *that's* over.

Vivian waits for me inside. I can feel her waiting, but I linger on, reluctant to leave the balcony and the darkness which hides my flushed cheeks and guilty thoughts.

The full moon brings out the worst in me. I am engrossed by trivia and pettiness, upset at the slightest thing.

It's not even my period.

Viv's period is looming. Thank God we don't bleed at the same time. It would be hell.

She'll be in a foul mood. And I'll have to grit my teeth and say yes Viv, no Viv, three bags full Viv. For at least three days.

'*You* wouldn't let me have a child!'

Viv is vigorously ticking my faults off on her fingers.

The nerve.

I take a deep breath. There is a critical second when I hover on the brink of either pacifying or ignoring her.

I am not dealing with a rational Viv. I am confronting a distorted, lying, whinging replica of my lover.

Even so. This idea has to be strangled to death before it festers further. A row has been brewing for days. I find myself diving in, boots and all. Self control flying recklessly out the window.

'You're so full of shit! *I*?' I beat my breast. '*I* wouldn't let you have a child?'

Vivian's knuckles gleam white on the table top.

'*You* couldn't make up your mind whose bloody sperm you'd deign to accept. *No one was good enough*!' I scream.

That shuts her up, for all of sixty seconds.

God knows why she is tormenting me like this, dragging up a subject that has been closed between us for at least five years.

'It wasn't that at all, and you know it. I didn't go through with it, because deep down, I didn't feel that the support was there from you.'

Our tongues have transformed themselves into venomous snakes, which slither about the kitchen with vicious intent . . . about to slash the two of us to ribbons.

'Don't lie to me. I *promised* that I'd back you up to the hilt if it was what you really wanted.' I remember her teaching, her committees, her book, her studying. All the achievements – the fine achievements she has behind her.

'That's what I *mean*. If *I* wanted. You didn't care one way or the other. It was just to please me – and now *it's too late*,' she whispers, tears streaming down her face.

There's only one thing left to do.

Go to bed.

'I had a dream last night,' says Vivian, hiccoughing.

'Did you?' I reply warily. She'll tell me anyway, whether I want to hear or not.

'I dreamed I had a baby.'

Shit!

'Golden-haired, with bright cheeky eyes and a tiny red rosebud mouth. She had so much confidence, that she could already speak.

'I was told that I had just given birth to her, but I couldn't remember doing so. I'd been so dreading the birth itself, that all I could feel, was a huge sense of relief that I'd been spared the knowledge of it.

'I went to stand up, but couldn't move. I reached down, trembling, to touch my vagina and my fingers came away wet and slick with redness. It was an open wound and I was bleeding like a pig.'

She lays her dreams down before me like an offering . . . a precious jewel.

I'm no doctor, no psychologist. I don't know any more how to deal with her. I have enough trouble trying to understand myself.

This dream is no jewel. It is a time bomb.

My heart is being plucked out by the roots.

I have no answers.

I first saw *you* at a party. I can't remember whose, and it wasn't the usual crowd. There were a few wimmin – butch and separate in one corner. I didn't know them and I didn't want to. People always tend to lump all of us dykes together, as if we're cut out of the same mould. But we're not.

For once, there were actually more men present than women. There were publishing people, a couple of journalists, a film-maker and a woman M.P. who always seemed to be surrounded. I don't know who the others were.

You really stood out.

It was quite deliberate, I'm sure. But strangely, you were alone. There was a clear space around you, so I could easily observe you, without making it obvious. Standing holding a martini, you appeared completely unselfconscious, as if it didn't bother you at all that nobody was talking to you. Your perfectly even teeth crushed the olive in a single bite.

You wore sunglasses. Pebble sunglasses, and I thought yes, very pretentious. *But* . . .

You wore black everything.

Black leather gloves. A black dress with long sleeves, a high neck and an odd skirt. A short burst of gathered taffeta fanning out over longer layers of tulle which fell to your ankles.

I can remember it all. The sheer black stockings and the black dancer's slippers.

You wore scarcely any make-up and looked pale and ill. A real night moth. Your dark hair was scraped simply back off your forehead and just cleared your collar.

I think I started to make my way towards you, but I never got there. Viv strode over and grabbed my arm in that very proprietary way she has and led me over to some balding language professor she wanted me to meet.

My heart went out to your aloneness.

When at last I extricated myself and searched for a final glimpse of black, there was no sign of you.

Your absence was like a blow to the stomach. I didn't even know you and already I missed you.

When I saw you three days later, I almost didn't recognize you. The sunglasses were gone and you were in jeans and a huge man's shirt.

Younger than ever.

You certainly didn't recognize *me*. You were buying a book.

Viv and I were making love.

I was paying a lot of attention to her breasts and her body was one long abandoned line of contentment.

Until I discovered the lump.

'Don't worry,' I say. 'It'll probably go away.'

Lies.

Viv cries. She doesn't believe me. She feels the lump for herself. The mood is spoilt and we don't finish our lovemaking.

She wants to discuss it to death.

Whoops – what am I saying?

'This is crazy. We've only just discovered the lump and in the last half hour you've already lived through two mastectomy operations. You're bald from chemotherapy. You've gone on to include cervical cancer . . . and if you carry on this ludicrous conversation, you'll have both of us dead, and the house burnt down by breakfast time. So shut up!'

I turn my back on her (which really pisses her off) and attempt to sleep.

She snivels behind me.

For God's sake.

I am not a hard-hearted bitch. I am not.

I might snap and snarl at Viv sometimes, and she at me, but really we're as happy as what do they say two bugs in a rug two little lovebirds.

Or were until I met you.

I have everything. You name it – I have it. So what more do I want?

What more indeed. The Garden of Eden before the Snake. A worm is eating at the apple of contentment. This very contentment has about it a blandness, a predictability that is beginning to irk me.

Yesterday, last week, last year, I was happy.

Today?

I am inventing you. This person I am hoping you will be. A spark is waiting to be lit. Girls who play with fire can be left with ashes.

I am walking with the dog boy's mother. We pass couples sprawled out face-down on the sand, under the shelter of the pohutukawas, reading newspapers. There are polystyrene chilly bins scattered about them.

The men and women seem very separate. There are fewer family units nowadays. People are too afraid to remember what it was like before.

Afraid to wonder what will happen when even the children die.

The dog boy shambles ahead of us, laughing and pointing at the sky, the crotch of his jeans fallen somewhere down around his thighs. I envy him his innocence.

He can't be left alone.

Something attracts his attention, and we catch him up. Seagulls. Dragging fish heads along the rocks and then lunging at them, swiftly hacking them to pieces. The dog boy's mouth is ajar, a slight dribble trickling from the gaping hole. Lee-Anne absently wipes his mouth with a Snowtex.

I have to turn away.

Lee-Anne with a gentle nudge urges him on. We pass the yacht club and settle ourselves on the top of the cemented rock retaining wall.

'*Do you ever have fantasies?*'

'Do I what?'

And Lee-Anne tells me:

'. . . I am sitting on a soft couch in an empty room. The walls are egg-shell blue and the ceiling is high. There is no furniture other than the couch, no paintings or ornaments, only a shiny tiled fireplace and an enormous round mirror hanging on the wall opposite me.

'I love the simplicity of it all. My mind floats and drifts. All my problems and cares have vanished. I am free to daydream.'

Lee-Anne's voice is low and pleasant. Soothing. Pitched over the years, to perfectly calm the dog boy. She could sedate him . . . If she wanted to.

Viv reckons she should have him locked up.

'Why?' I said. 'Just so *you* don't have to look at him? Or hear him. He's never done anyone any harm.'

'Yet,' said Viv.

Yet.

We saw him last night, pawing feverishly at the ground. We could hear the scraping sounds from the balcony where we were having a drink . . . *As if he were wanting to bury something.*

We leaned out over the trellis. He was lit up by the tiny lamp from their porch.

'He's no dog,' said Vivian.

I had to agree.

He looked more like a frog. And then we realized he was trouserless.

'My God,' whispered Viv in horror. 'I wouldn't want to bang into that on a cold dark night.'

Any night.

Lee-Anne shifts her position on the wall to get more comfortable. The dog boy is digging another hole.

'Go on,' I say. 'You are daydreaming . . .'

'I look at myself in the mirror. I have no nose or ears. I am all mouth and devouring eyes. My body is completely bandaged – except for my breasts. Each limb is separately wrapped in the softest . . . thinnest torn shards of silk. Draughts of wind blow around my exposed mouth and cunt.'

'. . . you and Helmut Newton. You and David Bailey,' I interrupt. Lee-Anne looks blank. She shushes me. I'm ruining the story.

'. . . the French doors are wide open. It is autumn and the wind is also blowing leaves into the room, great swirls of gold and scarlet and raw sienna. But I am not cold. There are large earthenware pots of tropical trees and plants flanking the edge of the tiled courtyard. And a single bush of apricot hibiscus swollen with blossoms of fiery crumpled tissue.'

I too see the courtyard and feel the wind on my skin, whipping my nipples into peaks. I see Lee-Anne, short, like the dog boy, reclining on the couch. His pug nose, on her, is pert. The same straw-coloured hair though and bright brown eyes. You would think Lee-Anne attractive, if you didn't always have to turn and confront her distorted mirror image.

The dog boy is scampering alongside an old lady wearing big black gumboots and holding a plastic bucket. She is detecting – swishing a gadget like the end of a vacuum cleaner across the sand. Listening intently through the headphones.

The dog boy is gesturing. He wants to do it too.

'. . . earless,' says Lee-Anne, 'I hear footsteps. It is the moment I have been waiting for. I stir expectantly in my bandages, which are neither constricting nor loose. I also hear whistling. The feet crackle on the dry leaves and seem to take an eternity to reach me. My fingers which are free, drum impatiently on my thighs. I catch a whiff suddenly, of smoke from a bonfire. Someone out there is burning fallen leaves.

'He fills the doorway. Noseless, I smell a delicious smorgasbord of outdoor scents: freshly mown lawn, sweat, tobacco, newly-dug earth, the roots of tender seedlings, the subtle smell of pine cones.

'He stands there for a long time staring at me.

'He bends down and gently removes my bandages. I can feel his warm

breath on my face, on my freed legs, my freed stomach, hips and arms.
My ears reappear. My nose becomes visible.

'I see all of this in my mirror.

'When I think I cannot bear the exquisite suspense any longer . . .
I leave my body.'

The dog boy is wearing the headphones and investigating the sand. I
know his eyes will be gleaming with joy. It takes so little. And yet,
where do women like Lee-Anne, and this old lady find the love and
patience it takes?

There must be something missing in me.

The dog boy jumps up and down and waves to us, trying to attract
Lee-Anne's attention.

'*Look Mum! Look at me.*'

Lee-Anne waves.

The dog boy links her to people, wherever they go. People who are
repelled, curious, amused. People who pity her. Children who tease
and point – *Look Mummy look at* . . . being shushed and dragged
away. Other people who simply – like this old lady – want to help.

The dog boy can be very responsive at these times. Surprisingly.

The sand is covered in footsteps. The hollows where hundreds of
feet have crossed and recrossed each other's paths during the day.

Sparrows peck cheekily at old sandwich crusts. Getting in, before
the sea gulls. The sea has the sheen of highly polished steel. There are
no waves – just ripples and eddies rimmed with brown.

The tide is on its way in.

'I become,' continues Lee-Anne, 'the man who is tormenting the woman.
I see her brown eyes riveted upon me and her hands which have been
touching me, flutter, sway and begin to touch herself. In all the tender
secret places I was saving for myself.

'I have never been so aroused, as becoming this composite
hermaphroditic being, touching and being touched. Entering and being
entered – all at the one time.'

Who is to say what is male? What is female?

'He and she and we and I are giddy drunk with this profane union.

'I replace the bandages with infinite care, wrapping each precious
limb in the softest . . . thinnest shards of torn silk.

'She/I sit bandaged on my couch. Only my tingling breasts are
revealed. Even my face has disappeared.

'Headless, I know he leaves.

'We have not exchanged a word.'

There is something that has disturbed me. Made me uneasy.

'. . . the bandages?' I say. I can't look at her.

We are silent for a moment. When she finally turns to me, her face is agonized.

We both stare at the dog boy, who is hovering about a windsurfer. The sail is going to come down.

In the late afternoon, the shadows are long. The sail as it tilts, forms a black thirty-foot Christmas tree along the sand. The dog boy runs to the end of the shadow and back again, laughing like a hyena.

'Why love with a stranger?' I ask curiously.

'It's the ultimate fantasy,' she says. 'To have a one-night stand now, is the same as playing Russian Roulette. Either of our lives could be endangered. I would be making love to all the partners he has had over the last decade.'

It must be frightening to be a heterosexual. Anyone could be a carrier of the disease – Aids. Almost everyone is at risk now.

'You dykes,' she says. But who isn't a dyke now? 'You'll be the last bastions of safe sex.'

Lee-Anne isn't the only one to be tied.

Vivian has been told she must have a biopsy at the hospital. After the operation she must wait two weeks to find out if she has cancer.

It hasn't been an easy time.

'Vivvie is afraid,' she whispered to me, in the middle of the night. Vivvie is what she calls herself when she is vulnerable, and so I used this name too.

'Vivvie is being unnecessarily pessimistic,' I replied. 'Think positive.'

'Your cheerfulness is getting on my nerves,' she snapped, with a flash of her old stroppy self.

Good, I thought.

But soon afterwards, she slumped and a few tears flowed.

'I dream about you,' she cried quietly.

I waited.

'I dream that you are leaving me.'

What could I say?

'Vivvie darling Vivvie don't cry. I love you, I think you're special. Of course I'll never leave you.'

This kind of thing.

Mush.

It is a litany.

'A celibate's dream, that's what my story is,' Lee-Anne laughs ruefully. 'What about you?'

What about me?

I wish I knew.

I begin to admit to Lee-Anne, my feelings for you . . . complicated feelings. The story of an obsession.

Perhaps your fascination for me, is your seemingly uncompromising flamboyance. We are not from the same world. Even the dog boy is more exotic than I.

'. . . I imagine a dress designer,' I tell Lee-Anne. 'Sarah. Dark-haired, pale-skinned and hot-tempered. I visit her salon. My patent leather shoes clattering across the polished floor. She is sitting behind a marblized table, head bent, hand-sewing a hem. I am very aware of the thunder of my high heels and the beating of my heart. I am torn between wanting to be invisible and at the same time feeling desperate that she notice me.

'She does. I have met her several times before, but never at her salon. She smiles her special triangular smile and after a few moments chatting, she leaves me to look around.

'It is not a welcoming interior. The salon is like a church. It feels sinful to speak louder than a whisper. Merchandise which is so expensive, inspires a certain reverence. Each dress is worth over a week's salary.

'The walls are white. All the fittings have been tampered with to falsely age them.

'Most of the clothes are black or slate grey. I am reminded again, of the first time I saw her. At a party.

'The dresses have big shoulders, high necks, long sleeves and tiny nipped-in waists. They are full enough and long enough to modestly cover both thighs and calves. They give an appearance of severity and austerity which is totally in keeping with the minimalist interior.

'I look out of place. These clothes are not me. They are for women who are sufficiently rich and bored to want to look like servants or missionaries. Quite confident in the knowledge that everyone will know the truth of the matter.'

'Would you like to try something on?'

'No . . . yes.' I don't want to offend her. To appear unappreciative of her designs. I grab the closest garment, my hands shaking. Awkward suddenly. Like a schoolgirl.'

I'd been with Viv so long, I no longer knew what to do, how to reach out to someone new. Someone like you.

' "I do have evening wear, you know. Come and look." She looks excited. I can tell she's very proud of her work. She's in her element.

'I smell the sweetness of her perfume and grip the garment tighter.

'I'm so wet, if I don't sit down soon I'll fall down. I think I should run out of the shop. I know I should.

'But I can't.

'Sarah leads me to a small enclave off the main salon which glows like an Aladdin's cave with satins, laces, silks, velvets and tulle.

'And so bright. It is like a peacock's garden after the starkness of the day wear.

'She pulls out a strapless boned dress in satin and tulle. Scarlet, lime and black. The skirt is decorated with large hand-made roses, loosely tacked on.

'Sarah leads me unresisting to the single changing-room.'

You don't talk much. You never do. Such a contrast to Viv, who is forever wanting to examine and dissect every little thought and mood. I long to fathom your silences, your sudden withdrawals into some secret place at the back of your head. Combined with the curiosity to divine your mystery, is the equally strong fear that behind the facade is . . . nothing.

You didn't expect to see me that day. Were your cheeks slightly flushed?

'I pull off my navy wool suit and cream silk shirt and attempt to squeeze into the gaudy concoction.

'Madness. I am due at a meeting in half an hour.

'The dress is so tight in the bodice I can't do it up properly. My breasts and hips, freed of the sensible suit, seem over-large and fleshy.

'I hear the salon door shut and then a click as the bolt is drawn.

' "How does it look?" She peeps through the oyster-coloured satin curtain and comes over to finish off the zip. My breasts spill over and I am left breathless.

'My face is aflame. I look like a whore. Unruly amounts of breast heaving lewdly under their confinement.

'I should rip it off immediately. And put on my suit.

'I've lost my head . . .'

'My God!' says Lee-Anne, choking.

She's laughing.

She wipes her eyes.

'That was no fantasy,' she states.

'No,' I admit reluctantly. 'It wasn't.'

The dog boy, thrilled to be outside amongst other people, bounds over towards a family who are walking below us looking for a suitable 'spot'. The man is carrying a very old lady in his arms, and stops – momentarily disconcerted at being confronted by the dog boy. He smiles uncertainly. He lowers her carefully into a folding chair and then places a yellow fluffy rug over her legs, tucks it around her pink cardy.

Soon, the mother, father and two children crouch on a small square tartan rug. The dog boy squats on the sand alongside them – fascinated. Out comes the thermos. A plate of pikelets is buttered, jammed and handed around by the mother. The old lady clasps the edge of a damp pikelet in a withered claw. Bony fingers pointed skywards.

The dog boy, always hungry (he eats Lee-Anne out of house and home), is in luck.

Who could refuse him?

'Anyway,' says Lee-Anne, getting back to the subject in hand. 'What are you going to do about it?'

It.

'I don't know.'

I who was once so certain, who had my life and career mapped out – successful, comfortably off. I feel increasingly these days, at a loss. A careless enraged child, kicking down and destroying building blocks she has so painstakingly built up.

I who have everything.

I peer miserably at the two discarded Coppertone bottles on the sand below me, at a crumpled Bluebird chip pack – as if they held the answers to my future.

In the distance, Rangitoto darkens as the sun little by little falls into the waiting sea. I cannot decipher the island's true colour – khaki, brown, slate grey, raw sienna or royal blue? Tiny white toy sails slice into its dark shape.

Soon it will be black and merge into a black sky.

I am oddly comforted by its permanence.

And what have I *not* told Lee-Anne?

I have not told her how even my dreams punish me.

I dream myself inside a church. I can hear the sweet murmuring voices of very small flower girls. I know without looking that they are wearing filmy chiffon veils and white lace dresses fastened with stiff sashes. They carry baskets of rose petals.

They file past me scattering white petals as they go.

I flee into the welcoming shelter of the confessional. I breathe a sigh of relief to be in its dark dampness.

I kneel down on the hard wood and cross myself.

'Bless me father,' I begin.

To my surprise I hear a familiar disapproving sniff. Have I said something wrong?

I continue.

'Bless me father, for I have sinned. It is many years since my last confession.'

I peer curiously through the fine wire mesh and can discern a familiar shape in the shadows. I hear a match being struck, and in the brief burst of flame I see Vivian. Breastless and stern, she puffs on her cigarette thoughtfully.

'Absolve me,' I beg.

There is an unforgiving silence from inside her booth. Outside the confessional, the flower girls are still singing softly. Only now, I can make out their words.

'. . . *Blood of my Saviour bathe me in thy tide.*'

Just a word. One little word is all I ask.

'*Mea culpa,*' I whisper. '*Mea culpa. Mea maxima culpa.*'

STEPHANIE JOHNSON

The Invisible Hand

The lights are on time release. I can flick the switch with my left hand while maintaining a hold on slippery Macha, and keeping the fingers of my right hand curled round the handle of the pushchair. Then we have precisely three minutes to get up the three flights of stairs, open the door – and there's always a struggle to find the keys – and get inside. Sometimes I have to leave bags of groceries at the bottom and must wait the two-minute time lag before I can flick the switch again, before the lights will come on, before I can get the groceries, and return to my Macha who by this time is removing every item of clothing from her round body including possibly soiled nappies, adding to the chaos. Chaos is a word my mother would use if she could see where we live, but she can't because she lives in New Zealand.

Macha and I don't go out much, except to the bank and the shops two or three times a week, and the park on the way to the post office. At the post office I clear my mail box. I run a kind of a business. Social Security doesn't know about my business, which is just as well.

The business wasn't my idea. Sometimes these things just appear, like gifts, or babies.

One night, before Macha could walk, I was lying down in the other room. It was winter and I felt just as dark and heavy as the rain outside. In preparation for times like this I had written helpful sentences on the wall around the bed.

I am Robyn – A Strong Woman
I am Robyn – Life-Giver and Mother
I am Robyn – Artist
I am Robyn – An Independent and Free-Spirited Woman

Tonight the phrases glance off my eyeballs. They don't even permeate to my brain, let alone my heart. Macha is crying and I hate her. She's been crying all day, one of her cheeks the bright red heralder of a new tooth. My sympathy for her has ebbed. Then suddenly, the phone rings.

I don't mind admitting I have few friends. My mother never phones. Sometimes Reece calls. Reece is the father of my son, and the judge gave him custody. Macha's father never phones. I only knew him for one night.

Macha stares at me, her mouth open but silent. Could it be that she already understands that telephones must be answered?

In the kitchen the floor is awash from the pissing washing machine. My thongs suck their way across to the bench.

'Hullo.'

There is nobody there. But just as I think about replacing the handset I discern a breathing. A breathing getting hoarser.

'Who is it?'

The breathing is interspersed with groans. There is a man coming, somewhere in the city, into my telephone.

I hang up loudly, in his ear. Macha uses the click as a cue to resume her yowling.

The next night is an action replay, although Macha's cheek is not so red and a tiny tip of tooth is presenting itself, and the man on the phone takes longer to come. I am surprised at myself for tolerating it. Perhaps I feel sorry for him. Men are so primitive, with it all hanging out of their bodies. At least I will not conceive from his attentions, through the ear, like an Elizabethan cat. And it is a good way to check that the phone still works.

My admirer calls most nights.

Then there is a day which is eventful. Macha takes her first steps, and sleeps that night exhausted. I am shunting the furniture around for something to do, when the phone rings.

'Hullo.'

There is complete silence, not even the breathing.

'Are you there?'

Of course, it needn't necessarily be the same bloke, I reason.

'You'll have to help me tonight.'

I am stunned – like a radio play with a lot of pauses I have finally heard his voice. He is American. Perhaps he is old.

'Can you hear me?' he asks.

'Yes.'

'The mind is willing, but the flesh is weak – do you get me?'

'Of course.' Although neither Reece nor Macha's father ever demonstrated this condition to me.

'Will you help me?'

'How?'

'Talk,' he says. 'Tell me what you look like.'

'Well, I'm . . .'

'Faster.'

'I'm tall, and I'm – I suppose I'm big, and –'

'What colour are your eyes?'

'Green.'

'Hair?'

'Brown.'

'How old are you?'

'Twenty-six.'

He comes. I put down the phone. I make a decision. The next time the phone rings late at night, I won't answer it.

Macha has to go to the doctor in half an hour. She keeps throwing up. I am hunting for the Medicare card, and loathing my predicament. I wonder if the receptionist will believe I have one if I tell her about it. The phone rings.

'Hullo.'

'You don't know me, but I've been calling you in the evenings.'

I am suddenly finely sprayed with water, from the inside, and my heart is thumping.

'I have a proposition to make. Are you interested?'

Macha covers the front of her jumper with green bile.

'I can't talk now. My kid is being sick.'

'You have a child?' He sounds disappointed.

'Two.' That ought to put him off.

'You are in need of a little financial assistance, then?'

What's he after? I'm frightened. Perhaps he knows where I live. I hang up.

But he doesn't let me get out the door. As soon as Macha is in a clean top he calls again. For the first time in . . . I can't remember how long, I'm angry.

'Leave me alone.'

'I'll give you five thousand dollars to start a club. There are other men who would use you.'

'What do you mean? Five thousand dollars?'

He laughs. He is American, he is a man, and he is obviously rich. He knows the power of money.

'A wanker's club.' I think he has what they call a Southern drawl. 'I belonged to one in the States.'

'What is it?' I asked. I pick Macha up.

'You get yourself a post office box. I'll send you the money. You'll have to advertise. Men will send you money and book a call. You'll learn business sense. Never accept a call without the money in your pocket.'

Macha is grizzling again. I am appalled at the degree of my temptation.

'Where do I advertise?'

'In any of the men's magazines.' He thinks I'm very stupid.

'Why are you doing this?' I ask. 'What do you get out of it?'

'I'll call back again.' For the first time he hangs up first.

I begin to dream. I dream of a car, nothing special, just a car. I dream of a little house for Macha and me. I picture an air ticket home to see my mother.

After we see the doctor I go to the post office to get myself a box. I tell the girl it's for 'The Invisible Hand Ltd', and I laugh. I spend a few dollars on a copy of *Ribald*.

Then, surprisingly, the American is true to his word. I open a bank account under my business name, and deposit the money. Macha and I have new clothes and I drive an old Volkswagen. I invest the rest.

One morning he rings me to tell me the ad is in *Ribald*. He is pleased with me, but disappointed that I haven't used my real name.

'You have more business sense than I thought,' he says. 'Where do you live?'

'It doesn't matter where I live.' Talking to this man is getting easier.

'Don't you think we should meet?' He hasn't sounded like this before – pleading, boyish.

'No.' I am firm.

In the first week I receive nine bookings, and they all ring. Some of them want to talk, but most of them are only interested in a swift ejaculation. I charge ten dollars a time. Business picks up to the rate of seven or eight calls a night, and Macha learns to sleep through the ringing.

At the end of the summer I put a deposit down on a little house.

To celebrate I invite two of the mothers from the park round for an afternoon cup of coffee. The kitchen is sunny, and I have made an effort to clean it up.

At four o'clock the phone rings. An early booking – it had completely slipped my mind.

'Aren't you going to answer it?' asks Sue, whose nose had wrinkled noticeably when she entered my home.

'No, I'll let it ring,' I say, stirring sugar into my coffee. 'I know who it is.'

'Who?' asks Frances, seated gingerly on a pile of newspapers. The copy of *Ribald* lies near her right foot. She hasn't noticed it.

'A business acquaintance,' I say. 'More coffee anyone?'

He hangs up. Sue and Frances look at each other meaningfully. Perhaps they think I'm whoring. Sue lights a cigarette, and I find her a saucer for the ash. She begins to tell us about her holiday up the Gold Coast with her man, when the phone starts again.

'Will you answer it this time?' asks Frances.

I do. I go through the whole act in front of them. This chap is a regular, and he needs a lot of coaxing. I coax him. Sue has flushed scarlet and is staring at me.

Then he is finished, and I put down the phone. Sue and Frances are statues of their former selves. The children babble in the bedroom.

'Oliver,' calls Sue. She is shoving her cigarettes into her bag. I notice she has woman-signs dangling from her ears. She goes into the bedroom, and through the open door I can see her reading my sentences on the wall.

Frances clears her throat.

'How can you do that?' she asks. 'Doesn't it make you feel sick?'

'Not really.' It had never occurred to me to feel sick.

Sue has Oliver by the hand. He has felt-tip all over his face, and it looks suspiciously like Macha's handiwork. She is glowering at me.

'I . . . um . . . I was a social worker before I had Oliver,' she says, all of the we-are-oppressed-women-together gone out of her voice completely, 'and I wonder if it isn't a good idea for me to take Macha with me now.'

'What? Why?' All the blood in my body is in my feet. If I'd known she was an ex-social worker I would never have invited her.

'You're unfit to be a –' she begins.

I am looking at her Gold Coast suntan. I am looking at this hole in the wall that I've made into a home for Macha and me ever since

Macha was born. I am thinking about Reece and Macha's father who was stronger than I was even though he was drunk. I am thinking about all these poor silly bastards who can't wank without a bit of help. I am so furious I have to laugh. Sue's biggest worry is balancing her heterosexuality with her politics. I know this because she told me.

'You're mad,' she's saying now. 'What are you laughing at? What you're doing is terrible – you have no need to do it – you're on the benefit aren't you?' There's a crack in her voice.

'Shut up,' Frances says to Sue. Slowly she gets up and comes across to me, smiling. She shakes my hand, collects her child, and pushes Sue and Oliver out ahead of her. At the door she turns.

'Is that how you got the house?' she asks.

I nod.

'Good on you,' she says.

I raise my coffee cup in a salute.

'I'm giving it up soon,' I say. But she's gone.

Macha and I are happy enough in our little house. We have a garden and a dog. There are no more phone calls but once a week I go into Grace Brothers and buy a dozen pairs of panties. The saleswomen are beginning to recognize me. Perhaps they think I have a panty fetish. I sell each pair for thirty dollars, after an hour's wear.

I wouldn't recommend my line of business for everyone. In a funny sort of way it's like the time-release lights in the stair well at our old place. Nothing lasts for ever.

On the wall in my new bedroom it says,

> I am a Strong, Free-Spirited Woman.
> I Control My Own Destiny.

HELEN WATSON WHITE

Two Worlds

It was a dream. It was all a dream, as they say. Or only. It was only a dream.

This dream crept up on me on a warm spring night with the scent of pear blossom hanging in the air. In fact it was such a warm, scented night that it was hard to tell what was dream and what wasn't. But somebody came and put ideas in my head, and draped their soft arms around my neck, and put a flower in the hair behind my ear.

It was a dream of soft women, like my mother, with the silky skin on the inside of her arms. They were walking the beach on an apricot evening, their long skirts billowing like sails – my mother, my aunts, my teachers with their 'never mind'. For no reason they appeared, walking the fine silt sand, their voices intertwining like garlands, open throats like flowers and a shell-like pearl in each eye. They sailed so serenely over the dunes, tiptoeing and gliding, they hardly seemed to be touching the ground. Sometimes one would go ahead of the others, and turn and throw up her arms to stop them, or bend with laughter as she told a story, wanting to gather them into it, wanting to address them all.

But what exactly she was saying I couldn't hear. It was melody, it was music, a song into the wind. And just as suddenly as they appeared on my mind-beach, circling and singing, they were gone. The waves danced whitely in their dream-like advance, lapping and laughing, covering the lazy slope of the dune with foam.

It would not perhaps have stayed with me, this dream-gift, if the morning had brought different news. If I had just walked to work past the pear tree and accepted its showers of foamy blossoms as an October reality. 'What sort of weekend did you have?' they would have asked. 'Oh I had a good weekend. Got lots done. Spent all Sunday in the garden actually.' Not saying how my heart had lifted as I turned the black earth where there were drifts of pear blossom between the rows. 'How did you get on? Did you get away?' I would ask in return.

But Monday's tide brought disaster. Some kind of monster was washed up and left lying like a root of kelp, rotting into the sand. The black headlines in the newspaper were thick like those kelpy stems: fat stinking and putrid though their outlines were hard.

'BOY DEAD AFTER PARTY' I read at the breakfast table. The paper was sodden, and stuck with petals from the path. The front page was dominated by an obscene photo of a mangled car. This was the real monster, it seemed to imply – no humans in sight. But somebody had been driving it. It was Ken, but he was dead now. Roger and Valerie's Ken. The next of kin would have been notified.

I remembered the party in the Castle Street flat where Roger first met Val, where he had taken me a few times. They had to get married – after another party, not that one. I was better out of it. I didn't mind. Roger would have been nineteen then. Ken was only a sixth-former now.

It was only one of many flats – all those villas with a hall down the middle, all close to the ground on their wooden piles, all sunk into earth, all the same. But I remembered the inside of it as if it were yesterday: the dark panelling along the hallway, the two glass-fronted bookcases by the rubbish-filled fire. It was the front bedroom by the street, behind the hydrangeas, that had the best stereo. That was Col's room when I was going out with Roger. I don't know why I liked Roger better than Col. He had no stereo, no car, and no brains either. Just a big grin and strong forearms. I imagine Ken was just the same.

'*Five others injured, two seriously.*' I didn't recognize their names. I felt sick remembering Roger tussling with me on the narrow bed in his small side room. Full of beer, full of bonhomie. Smiling as he stroked my hair, but then gripping me with both hands, pressing himself into my side. I feeling affection, and fear, and an awful ambivalence about his warmth which seemed to invade me even through our clothes. The only way I could repel him was by having him on. I was fairly strong myself, but I could never have prevented him if he really wanted to push himself home. I had to scoff and joke and laugh him down.

Val couldn't do that, apparently. And she certainly wasn't on the pill, being a good Presbyterian country girl. How must she be feeling? Even with her two other sons. She'd made a go of it, after a bad start.

Roger wasn't all that bad I suppose. He's not a bad father, either, at least at weekends. I've seen him with the two younger boys coming away from the rugby grounds. I live near there. But I seldom see Val. Or Ken, for that matter. From the sound of it he leads his own life, with a borrowed car. He gets around. They do it earlier and earlier these days.

They are school-kids at most of the parties near my place. The students are away skiing. I see them setting off when I walk home from work on a Friday night, bang into them coming out of the bottle-store with supplies. They make me feel like a peasant or a pauper even though I'm not. It's just that I have to carry all my groceries and library books and I find it easier in a back-pack. I'm always carrying something because I don't have a car. I figured it was better to buy a house, and I love it, though there's a bit of a noise problem down our end.

And now this. It doesn't say where the party was. Just that the car hit a lamp-post in Cumberland Street, on the driver's side. For God's sake, the street is one-way, completely empty at two o'clock on a Sunday morning, and as wide as a football field. How the hell did he end up on the footpath? And where were they going, the six of them? Where was there to go?

I remembered driving out to St Clair in the back of Col's Vauxhall, getting out and running down the sand-hills in the dark. All of us tripping over each other and grabbing at jerseys, the boys robust with beer and sweating hotly, making a lot of noise with few words. Opening their arms to the sea, declaiming obscenities or platitudes. The girls would be giggly, sweetened with wine that if it had spilt down the side of their glass was still sticky on their hands. We didn't put our arms around each other but went for the boys, though they hardly noticed which one was tugging at them, dragging round their necks, flinging herself at them with no head but a mane of thoughtless hair. They took it for granted, like everything else: the wide street lit with an empty orange light, their freedom, the sea.

We were blind and dumb, we girls, and forgiving to the end. Clearing up the mess after parties, stacking the bottles, wrapping up the glass. For what? For the privilege of appearing of an afternoon at a friend's place with a man's arm around our shoulders. Of being told we were okay. Of being taken for granted like milk and fresh eggs, or the waves that perpetually stroked the beach at St Clair.

We nourished these boys in their simplicity. We taught them they didn't need to mind. I could have been Roger's mother as Val was Ken's, the way I indulged his vacancy, tending the hole in the zero – the gap of awareness where he should have been. I could be Ken's mother. It could be my boy that died.

That killed himself, I should say. That propelled his body against a fixed and immovable object, sending the neurons scattering at the speed of sound. That murdered the day for the five others, and brought blankness and horror to our living-rooms. An act of violence against us, this spring night suicide; only he had oblivion for a balm.

I gathered myself to go to work as best I could, and asked the others if they'd seen the news. Ken Fraser, I said, Val and Roger's boy.

But no, they said, this was another one, connected with a Port Chalmers family. They could tell by his middle name. Dotty knew that's what his spinster aunt was called.

I was silent. I took it back. 'Oh.' But then I thought: What difference does it make? This one, that one, another one. The characters in the scene were interchangeable; I could have been one of them a few years ago . . .

I might have been the girl in the back seat who said nothing when the driver went too fast, veering crazily round corners, accelerating on an uncertain path. Who merely shut her eyes and stayed invisibly where she was, cuddled under the arm of a boy who blurted 'Go for it Ken!' (or Roger or Kevin or Col) 'Show us what you're made of!' – and the others would chorus, slurring their words: 'Don't be a girl . . .'

Who would be a girl, I thought, to live in the aftermath. To pick up the broken bottle from the path. To lift the broken thoughtless head. To wash the blood from the hand-knit jersey, to knit the jersey that would be bloodstained . . .

It didn't bear thinking of.

So why was I thinking about it? I decided I wouldn't spare it any more energy, just because I was alive.

I also decided to get in touch with Val, but I wouldn't mention the accident. We don't have to go along with it, I thought. We don't have to live in their world. Let them get their own shit together. Let them clear up their own bloody path.

Val has her own life, and I have mine. She has a garden, I know – I've seen her weeding in the front beds a few times. So we've got something in common. Blossom. Pear blossom. Blossom between the rows.

CARIN SVENSSON

Eight for Eternity

School in the morning. Helen sucked her pencil and wrote with even letters 'Mother is kind. Father walks the dog.' Annemarie scratched her ankle, chewed at a fingernail and hissed in Helen's direction, 'How do you spell *walks*?'

Farm in the afternoon. Late autumn came. Early winter. Down by the creek. They were wearing gumboots and thick jackets. On her head Annemarie had a grey knitted cap with a pompom on top. She looked like a small leprechaun darting this way and that, in the middle of the streaming water. They were building a dam.

Hands freezing cold. Their mittens lay discarded on the bank. Fingers red and numb, they were lugging boulders around in the water.

'Put that one next to the round one!' yelled Annemarie in a loud voice wanting Helen to hear her across the rushing water. She pointed with the finger whose nail was chewed off.

Helen dropped the big boulder in the appointed place. The water splashed into her boots and she shrieked. She bent down to manipulate the stone in order to tighten the dam.

The water was brown and muddy. The grass on the banks not green any longer, but yellow and tufty. The grey sky above. It was late afternoon and quietly it started to snow.

'Hey, look! The first snow,' screamed Helen and jumped about trying to catch snowflakes with her hands. 'The first snow!'

Annemarie with her grey head bent down over her stone wall pointed, 'That square one now!'

A car drove past on the road. A truck with a hook behind the cabin. Annemarie looked up at last.

'Come on!' she yelled. 'That's the butcher.'

'The butcher?' asked Helen with apprehension. 'What's he going to do?' She clambered after Annemarie who was disappearing over the top of the bank. Clonk, clonk their gumboots went on the road. Towards the cowhouse.

At the other end, close to the stable, came Annemarie's father. Together with Andersson he was dragging the big pig forward. She was more grey than pink. Her big ears flopped sadly as she tried to turn the other way. But the two men in their blue dirty pants and long muddy gumboots kicked her into the right direction. Even Annemarie's father gave her short angry kicks.

'Move, move!' he yelled in an unfamiliar falsetto voice.

There stood the truck with its ominous hook and there was the butcher with his shining face and strange-looking gun in his hand.

The boys on the farm were there, too. All the kids stood in a silent row next to the box-like enclosure into which the fat flabby pig had been forced. She stood with her sides trembling like jelly, she put her snout up and sniffed the air. Her trotters moved on the floor.

Helen took a deep breath. Involuntarily she grabbed for Annemarie's sleeve and let her hand stay there in a tight grip.

Annemarie's father nodded to the butcher, who put a contraption over the pig's head and pointed the gun into it from above. There was a muffled bang and the pig collapsed on to the side of the box. She didn't even squeal. Her legs shook and kicked and the mass of flesh slid down on to its side.

Helen looked at Annemarie. She tugged at her sleeve. She wanted to cry. Throw herself on the dirty floor. Kick and yell. The pig, the pig, that she hated while she was alive, lying on her back in the muddy yard, turning and twisting, making herself dirtier and dirtier. Smelling foul and sounding worse. She hated the pig. But now the butcher had shot her and without wanting to the pig had lost all control. With a heavy hump she had fallen against the wooden boards that creaked. The legs with its helpless trotters kicking and kicking in the air. OOOH, for the heavy helpless mass of dirty pig.

Annemarie didn't take any notice of Helen. She sucked her lip and her chin looked larger than usual. She took a grip of her woollen cap and pulled it down further.

'Let's go down to the wash-house,' she muttered.

Helen didn't question her this time although she wondered why the wash-house.

It stood down by the creek. The smoke rose from its chimney. Inside there was boiling hot water, steaming out of the open door into the frozen air. The snowflakes melted as they were caught by the steam. On the ground all around lay a thin cover of snow. Their feet made dark prints they didn't have time to see.

Inside the wash-house in the light from the naked bulb, in the billowing steam stood Annemarie's mother. She had an old jersey on, buttoned in front with the torn sleeves rolled up. On top of her dark skirt she wore a flowery apron that had seen better days. She held a glinting sharp knife in her hand.

Annemarie and Helen waited next to a couple of zinc buckets by the door. They knew they had to be quiet and keep out of the way. It was the expression on the face of Annemarie's mother. Solemn and the eyes unusually black.

There came her husband with the pig. On a wheelbarrow. He ran down the slope towards the wash-house. The pig was bigger than him. Her legs hung over the edge, they dangled in rhythm to his steps.

Annemarie's mother stood ready with the knife.

'Over there,' she ordered, the knife pointing to the hook, where she wanted the pig. They levered her up together. The pulley wailing in sympathy for its heavy load.

Annemarie's father rested for a while with his hands on his hips. His unconscious smile returned. He seemed relieved that his part of it was over. When he took off his glasses and wiped his damp forehead with the back of his sleeve, it left a dark smudge over his eyebrows.

'I'll leave it to you then.' He nodded to Annemarie's mother who didn't hear him. She had already stuck the knife into the neck of the pig.

'Don't stand too close!' he said to Annemarie and patted her on the head. 'You might get your pompom chopped off.'

He winked at Helen, who wished he would stay, before he disappeared up the path, bent over the wheelbarrow.

The blood almost black welled out of the pig into a zinc bucket. Annemarie's mother held it ready just in time. The steaming blood flowed.

Now she scooped up some flour out of a sack by the door and poured it into the blood. Then she whisked. She whisked and whisked. The blood frothed and turned pink. Her strong arms that came out of the torn woollen sleeves got splattered with droplets of blood and drops were projected out on to the thin layer of snow.

There hung the pig quivering. The steam and the blood and the big hunk of pig. And Annemarie's mother working frantically. She started to cut and chop with a sharp-bladed small axe that swung up and down.

'Oh, God, let it stop,' thought Helen.

The mother was a witch with her brewing kettles. The wash-house enveloped in smoke, steam and blood. The snow kept falling, blood seeped into the creek in dark little streams. The pig wasn't a pig any more. Her guts had been torn out to be cleaned for sausages. They hung from a branch in a tree nearby. Her blood had been whipped, her trotters cut off. And the ham for Christmas. Oh, the ham for Christmas, how could she ever taste it again. With mustard on. No, no!

The mother was a witch and Annemarie, her daughter, a leprechaun struck by the first ray of sun. Still as a stone. Helen tugged at her arm and said 'Annemariiiiie' as loud as she dared.

But Annemarie was looking at her mother with an expression where disbelief and admiration mingled. She didn't hear. Only her eyes moved. They followed the movements of the axe. Up and down.

Helen felt ill at ease. For once she was homesick, longing for Mother at the piano with the candles lit. The flames vibrating slightly as Mother touched the keys.

'Bye,' she said and thumped Annemarie on the arm. She climbed up the path to her bike and rode it against the dark wind blowing snowflakes into her nostrils. Back to home where she hoped for vegetable soup and pancakes.

The days went by. At school they talked about Bethlehem. The Shepherds and the Kings. The Star. Teacher helped them make a model of the Manger. Helen's job was the Donkey. In clay. It's ears grew. It looked like an Easter Bunny and wasn't in proportion to Baby Jesus. Teacher didn't mind.

'Well done, Helen!' she said. 'We'll put it here as a backdrop.'

Christmas came and Helen forgot all about the pig. She asked for several slices of ham and put them on a piece of rye bread thickly spread with mustard. Somehow she didn't connect the grey dirty mountain of trembling pig on the wash-house floor with the clean pink ham she was putting her teeth into.

However, she looked at Annemarie's mother in a different way. Her name was Astrid. It fitted. The heavy eye-brows and dark eyes. Hands that kneaded, lifted and spun. The broad shoulders.

Helen's own mother often relied on Astrid for help in the vicarage. For the spring clean or when the bishop came for inspection and a big dinner had to be prepared.

In late winter when the afternoons were already lighter, but still bitterly cold, Astrid came to put up the loom. A large wooden loom, roughly made. You could see where the axe had cut. Only the seat had been worn down to a smooth shiny surface.

Astrid came alone. Annemarie didn't care much for the huge vicarage with all its rooms. The thick bible large as a small coffee table lying open, spread out, ready to be read at any time. It made her nervous.

But Astrid was the same anywhere. The same in the light from the electric bulb in the steamy wash-house as in the spacious vicarage. She took away the curtains from the window in Mother's room where the loom was to stand.

'You need all the light you can get,' she stated and unhooked them.

She placed different pieces of wood and long shafts belonging to the loom into different piles, oblivious of the group of three looking on. Mother and daughters – Maria, who was older, and Helen. She muttered to herself. Words that they hadn't heard before. They waited patiently, looking at Astrid's strong hands moving and rattling the wooden pieces here and there.

'You know we want to help,' said Mother timidly.

Astrid mumbled something about 'The Devil take this one . . .' and didn't hear. Mother looked at Maria and Helen. She made her eyes roll in a funny way. The girls tried it too until they giggled all three. They were sisters together. Astrid was Mother Strict.

She called Mother, Missus, and her voice wasn't quite as dark as before. It appeared she treated Mother differently. With kid gloves, as the saying went.

'Well Missus, let's see what we all can do.'

Astrid instructed them. Her mood had changed now that all the pieces were sorted and nothing amiss. She didn't mutter, but was calm and methodical with all three of them.

'Now, like this. Pull that one. Not like that, like this. Hold tight now. And push.'

Father took a break from the office. Came in and tapped with the hammer on some of the bits of wood. Astrid looked on and something of a smile played in the corner of her mouth, or perhaps it was a tick.

'Thank you, Vicar,' she said in her alto voice again.

It took a few hours. Then the loom stood there complete with the long round shaft where the new cloth was to be wound and stretched by moving the iron rod with its teeth. The black teeth in Astrid's hand reminding Helen of the slaughter. The blood and the sawn-off trotters. Through a curtain of snowflakes. Astrid on centre stage swinging the axe with the glinting edge. The pig.

Astrid looked at her knowingly. Did she know what went on in Helen's head.

'We've been through a bit you and me, hey?' She gave Helen's plait a quick sharp tug.

'Coming to play with Annemarie tomorrow aren't you?'

Helen felt warm inside. Astrid had never touched her before. It had hurt a little, but she knew it was a sign of fondness. Like when boys at school tried to pinch the girls.

'Next fine day we'll do the warp,' said Astrid. She left the question why it had to be fine hanging unanswered.

On one of the very early spring days, when there was still a chill in the air but a lightness underfoot showing that the frost had loosened its grip in the ground, Astrid decided that it was time for the warp.

The four of them went down to the southerly side of the old empty stable by the church. Astrid hammered in some nails at both ends of the wall and walked with the yarn from one end to the other, hooking it on to the nails.

It had to form the shape of an eight. They followed the pattern between the nails walking along the warm red wall. Helen did it too with the yarn slipping between her fingers until her hands became red and sore. Blisters formed. Maria took over.

Astrid watched everything, not missing a single twist of the yarn. She stroked a strand of grey hair away from her face and narrowed her eyes against the sun.

Annemarie wasn't there. She would have been restless. She would be with her father buying grain, or walking through the cowhouse with Andersson's son, looking at the black stallion nervously stamping his hooves on the straw.

Helen missed her a little. But now when Mother and Maria were learning to weave she wanted to be part of it. She was proud to be allowed. It meant that she was the same as them. She'd be a woman too, sitting on the worn seat of the loom. Throwing the shuttle from right to left between the see-through wall of cotton yarn. A mouse rushing through a secret tunnel. Caught at the other end. Snug in her hand. Thump the yarn in place with a couple of firm beats of the reed. Down with the clunky treadle under her foot. Everything creaking and clattering and back to the shuttle again.

Now they were walking the warp. In the sun, from end to end of the warm red wall. A path formed in last year's yellow grass.

Mother's turn. The sky above pale blue. They hummed in rhythm to their steps. Now and then reminded by Astrid that this was supposed to be work. Serious work.

'Watch the nail, girl,' she warned.

All the yarn sitting on the wall. A long horizontal eight, for eternity, creamy white on the dark red wall.

The moment when Astrid carefully lifted off the yarn: She stuck her hand shaped into a hook inside the yarn and made a loop. She pulled and twisted her hand with the yarn around it and formed another loop. It looked like magic.

> *Two crows beaks in a kettle of pig's blood.*
> *A twisting snake. Put the hex on it.*
> *Bubble and sizzle. Stir it and whisk it.*

Simsalabim and she looped up all the warp into one long braid. A gigantic wheaten length ready for the oven. Now it could easily be handled.

By Easter the fabric had grown. The iron rod with its teeth had already been used several times to roll up the cloth. It grew unevenly, dense or loose depending on the weaver and the weaver's mood.

The beginning was even. That was Astrid's part. She sat firm, her bottom in the same place, only arms and legs moving. She kept a steady rhythm going for hours.

Helen's part of the fabric was usually denser than the others.

She wove when she was alone at home. Perched high on the worn seat. Her arms were too short, she slid from side to side in order to reach. She hit hard with the reed, she knew the warp could take it. Thump, thump. How strong she was. Then loosely throw the shuttle. The gentle touch now, otherwise it would fly out the window. The foot on the treadle. Clunk. She had to slide forward to reach. It was like a sitting-down dance with arms and legs, bottom and hands.

There she sat. Just like other women. She ruled her domain, she was in control, this was her throne.

She wanted to be like Astrid. At least a little. But Astrid was so different. She came from another world, solid and dark. Where the colour of earth tinted all. It smelt safe and warm, but also bottomless like whiffs of chilly air from the deepest hollow of the cellar. A witch surrounded by all the steam in hell at the slaughter. A wise old woman with her trollsticks at the loom.

And what with Annemarie, her daughter? On the outside she was her father's child. She followed him, learnt from him. But she went to it with the same deep intent as Astrid. In the creek shifting stones for the dam, closing the gate behind the bull or burning the dead grass after harvest.

Helen and Annemarie sent each other cards for Easter. They had painted them at school. On Helen's card from Annemarie was a big fat hen with a minute yellow chicken next to her. From the hen's beak there was a speech balloon saying 'Happy Easter'.

Annemarie had already watched with envy when Helen painted her card with bright colours from the paintbox in the corner of the classroom. It was a bunch of naked branches put together in a vase. On the branches were attached hens' feathers dyed in bright orange, red and blue. On one of the branches a small note was attached. 'Happy Easter to Annemarie from Helen'.

Biographies

Janet Arthur: I was thrilled to hear you liked my story as it is the first of many I hope to write. I am a thirty-two-year-old mother of three who has always wanted to write. I found the courage to begin writing only after I opted out of a ten-year marriage. This story is based on some of my own experiences as a teenager. As a recovering alcoholic I have only now overcome the trauma which these experiences created.

Cherie Barford: Born 1960 of European/Polynesian descent. Lives in Auckland where she relief-teaches and performs poetry in pubs, cafes and secondary schools. Published in NZ journals, *Ariel, Landfall, A Plea to the Spanish Lady* (her own book of poetry). Loves music, reading, writing, dancing and Persephone – her cat.

Lucinda Birch: I was born in 1962 and grew up on a farm in the Wairarapa. I spent three years at Ilam School of Fine Arts majoring in photography and left before completing my degree. I started writing a few years ago after travelling nine months and seeing so many other tourists take so many photographs that I couldn't even pick up my camera. And then it got stolen. I now live in Greytown and divide my time between making up, taking and painting photographs (with my new camera), writing, and weeding. These are the first stories I have had published.

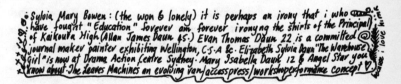

Sylvia Mary Bowen: (the won & lonely) it is perhaps an irony that i who have fought "Education" forever am forever ironyng the shirts of the Principal of Kaikoura High (Allan James Daun 45.) Evan Thomas Daun 22 is a committed journal maker painter exhibiting Wellington, C.S.A & Elizabeth Sylvia Daun "The Warehouse girl" is now at Drama Action Centre Sydney. Mary Isabella Daun 12 & Angel Star you know about. The Leaves Machines an evolving van/accesspress/workshoperformance concept ♥.

Francis Cherry: No academic qualifications. Was afraid that if she tried she might fail but if she didn't who knows? Parents were well-known Communists so she lived in her own world most of the time, only coming out to entertain people. In her creative writing classes she sees the damage that has been done to people by the education system and is glad she escaped. Her education came after leaving school, through WEA and other continuing education courses. Even though her mother was a strong, intelligent, feminist woman, Frances married young, had five children and spent most of the time, against great odds, trying to tell herself she was happy. She has never regretted leaving her marriage and has found life since then unpredictable, sometimes traumatic, but always exciting and full of wonder. She has had stories published in literary magazines, radio, school journals, three anthologies, and her own collection (*The Daughter-In-Law And Other Stories*, New Women's Press 1986). A novel, *Dancing With Strings*, is coming out this year (NWP). Lives in Wellington with fifteen-year-old daughter, Caitlin, a flatmate, one dog, two cats and her mother downstairs.

Terry Driessen is thirty-two years old and lives in Auckland. She has had a range of jobs from fish process worker to Treasury economist – and more recently, newspaper proof reader. 'Curious Perspective' is her first short story; she hopes to publish more.

Annabel Fagan: I am a middle-yeared woman and have a fifteen-year-old son, Joshi. We live with Jotter 4 (dog) and Daffodil 8 (cat) and find our family a satisfying one. I like labels. I live in Auckland but am Wellington-born and love that city passionately. Real Estate was my last place of work and I have no regrets about leaving. I hate sexism and racism and have no time for heterosexuals, who when I tell them I'm a lesbian, say, we don't mind Annabel.

Paula Green lives in Auckland, has recenty finished a novel and begun work on another. She is anticipating a move to another foreign city.

Arapera Hineira: I am a descendant of the tribes of Ngati Porou, Ngati Kahungunu, Rongowhakaata, Te Aitanga-a-Mahaki. I was born in Rangitukia on the East Coast, ten miles south of the East Cape. I enjoy words that sparkle, whether they be Maori, my mother tongue, or English. What a privilege it is to inherit and to appreciate a language, and to enjoy another equally.

Stephanie Johnson: I was born in Auckland in 1961 and have written for as long as I can remember. I began publishing my work in Christchurch in 1979. I particularly enjoy writing about women of all kinds. I write poetry (*The Bleeding Ballerina*, 1987), plays (*Accidental*

Phantasies, 1984–85) and short stories (*The Glass Whittler*, 1988). Since coming to Australia in 1985 I have also been writing film and T.V. Previously I worked as an actress in both Sydney and New Zealand.

Jan Kemp: Born 1949 Hamilton, graduated M.A.(Hons) from the University of Auckland in 1974 and since then has lived mostly outside New Zealand, but on the fire rim of the Pacific Ocean.

Presently she teaches English language at the National University of Singapore and is writing poems, short stories, critical articles and a novel.

Her three publications to date, *Against the Softness of Woman*, 1976; *Diamonds and Gravel*, 1979; and *Ice-Breaker Poems*, 1980 are all out of print. Most recently she is represented in the *Penguin Book of New Zealand Verse*, 1985; the *Oxford Anthology of Twentieth Century New Zealand Verse*, 1987; as well as *New Women's Fiction edited by Cathie Dunsford*, 1986, and *SPAN* 1987 and 1988.

Anne Kennedy: Born 1959 in Wellington and studied music at Victoria University. Lives in Auckland. Script-writer and writer of short fiction.

Judy McNeil: Some people paint QT on their legs when they're fifteen to create a fake tan. It took me 'til I was thirty-seven to do it. This is how it is with writing. I started at thirty – short silly poems which eventually became more developed with practice. I set out to write a book. I have been distracted over the last few years from my original purpose but have ended up with quite a few short stories, two plays, and heaps of poetry, mostly unpublished. I've mostly used my writing for performance.

Heather McPherson: Born 1942 Tauranga. Involved since 1974 with feminist/lesbian politics, arts/literary projects (including *Spiral* women's arts magazine and The Women's Gallery). Also write poems (two books), book reviews, articles and lately prose; spent four years enmeshed in patriarchy whence emerged with house in coastal village where live semi-quietly with son, cat and dog, and assorted fruit trees.

Fran Marno: I am forty-one and live in Auckland with my daughters Larissa (14) and Joanna (11). I spent a year at art school in 1983 and came across sexism that was so blatant and debilitating that my feminist consciousness was raised at great speed. For four years now I have painted on my own. It's exciting but not easy. More recently, writing has become a way of exploring the issues and contradictions in life that I struggle to contract into single visual statements in my painting.

Being a mother, a lesbian, a painter and a writer provides me with challenges that I plan to keep alive and work with for at least another forty years.

Suzi Pointon was born in Wellington, New Zealand. She studied fine arts at Auckland University, film directing at the American Film Institute in Los Angeles and screenwriting at the Australian Film and Television School in Sydney. Since the late 1960s she has worked in film and theatre in New Zealand, Australia, France, England and the United States. She has had stories published in Australia and was a finalist for three years in the Australian/Vogel literary award.

Currently she is living with her husband and two sons in Parkersburg, West Virginia, where they are making a television series on Appalachian folklore. She is also working on a novel about the Kiwi ghetto in Sydney.

Wendy Pond grew up in the Hinuera district of the Waikato. She is a scholar of Austronesian languages and a member of the Entomological Society. She won the 1987 BNZ Katherine Mansfield Short Story Award.

Barbara Rea: I was born in Ireland in 1950 and first came to New Zealand fifteen years ago. I earn my living as a lecturer in law. 'Story' was one of the returns from a women writers course I took as part of a wider programme of reclamation.

Sue Reidy: I graduated from the Wellington Polytechnic School of Design at the beginning of 1976. I have worked full-time as a graphic designer/illustrator ever since, both here and overseas. I have been a partner in a design practice for the past six years and have designed and illustrated many NZ book covers. Travels in S.E. Asia have been a major source of inspiration for my work – both in the graphics and writing fields. I've written spasmodically for the past fifteen years. I won the 1985 BNZ Katherine Mansfield Short Story Award. My stories have been published in *The Listener* and my first collection of short stories entitled *Modettes* is being published by Penguin Books this year. I am also designing and illustrating the book.

4

77157

Elizabeth Smither is the author of seven collections of poetry and two novels; she is also a journalist, critic and librarian. She has recently begun writing short stories.

Marvynne Sotheran: I was born in Stratford, Taranaki, grew up in remote country areas where my parents were teachers. Secondary education was at St Mary's College, Ponsonby, followed by Auckland University (B.A. in English) and Secondary Teachers' College. I've been married (am not now), had three children, and taught, mainly English, in New Zealand and now, in Melbourne, Media Studies. I've lived three years in Australia, hope to return to New Zealand soon. I've been writing seriously only for about eighteen months, have submitted very little (one novel, several stories) for publication, but this will be the first story I've had published. (So you can see why I'm happy!) I want to continue to write – I'd like to write film scripts – as much as I can to make up for lost time.

Carin Svensson: I was born in Sweden in 1942 and came to New Zealand in 1969. As a single parent with one child, working part-time as a librarian and translator, I now find more time to write than before. And that's good!

Ngahuia Te Awekotuku writes that she can't contain all her selves within a single sentence . . . but at first sighting, is a middle-aged Maori lesbian, with a fiendish weakness for cats. And chocolate, dark, rich, and bitter.

Cynthia Thomas: I live in Whangarei, am fast approaching thirty, and attempt to teach secondary school English for a living. I grew up in the North, spent five years at Waikato University, one at Auckland Teachers' College and two in Europe (where outrageously lax typing jobs allowed me many hours to practice writing). I have been writing short stories every now and then since I was ordered to at secondary school, and apart from a couple of stories in the university newspaper, have never had anything published. (But I was a *really* good Pixie Page contributor for the New Zealand Woman's Weekly as a child, and won many points for poems about flowers swaying in the breeze, and drawings of obscurely shaped cats up trees etc – are you *sure* this doesn't count???)

Helen Watson White (born 1945) is a writer, editor, performer and critic with a special interest in the theatre of Aotearoa. Her poetry and fiction have been published in *Review, Landfall* (winning in 1984 a runner-up short fiction prize), *Broadsheet* and *Untold*. Her theatre and book reviews appear regularly in *The Dominion/Sunday Times* and her work may be heard on the radio in story and diary form.

Rawinia White: I was born in rural South Auckland in 1955 of Maori (Ngati Awa) and Pakeha ancestry. I have lived most of my life in Auckland. Whakatane is my papakainga. Although I have never lived there, wherever I go my wairua remains there with that of my ancestors. The last two years have been a voyage of rediscovery for me. I began writing during this time to express and record my experiences, both for myself and for other people who may find something in my stories.

Aorewa McLeod: Born in Auckland in 1940, I have taught English Literature at the University of Auckland since 1970. Since 1980 I have taught a course on Twentieth Century Women Writers. I will never again edit another collection of stories as I found the process of selecting too agonizing – I hated eliminating fine stories and would wake up in the early morning hours worrying over my choices and my standards. I'm an out lesbian and a closet writer and my ambition is to have a story in the next *New Women's Fiction* collection.

Kathryn Madill: I was born in Ruatahuna in 1951 and later lived in Taupo and Dunedin. Graduated in 1971 from Ilam School of Arts and then lived in Nelson, Waikouaiti and Dunedin, printmaking and painting. I currently live in Auckland.

A third *New Women's Fiction* anthology will be published in 1989. Please submit your stories by 30 September 1988 to: New Women's Fiction, New Women's Press, P.O. Box 47-339, Auckland.